BETTER BONES AND GARDENS

PERSEPHONE PRINGLE COZY MYSTERIES: FOUR

PATTI LARSEN

Thanks, Kirstin!

ISBN: 978-1-989925-79-9

CHAPTER ONE

I'd be the first to tell you the interior of Vesterville House was about as creepy as they came, the massive, old mansion more an Americanized castle with its dark stained wooden interior and endless dim corridors lined with staring and judging ancestors who I always felt wanted me to leave and never come back.

No matter how many times I visited, things never improved. Which made me wonder why my daughter, Calliope, loved it there. Of course, the fact her girlfriend owned the place and choosing to call Vesterville House home meant they could be together probably had a lot to do with it.

Dunno. Love was powerful, but. If love called me to live there? Heck to the no. Not powerful enough under any circumstances in my opinion. I guess that meant my daughter was braver than me and she could have that victory.

The grounds of the estate, on the other hand? A far and away cry from the stuffy, supernatural feel of the supposedly cursed estate house (Thalia Vesterville's words, not mine). Dare I say, the surrounds reflected the finest and most of appealing designs and demeanor that Mother Nature had to offer. Refreshingly alluring, the cultured parkland punctuated by winding pathways of patterned cobblestones led to delicate private scapes where one could sit and ponder the meaning of life while breathing in fresh air and the scent of exotic flowers, as if the entirety of mankind had vanished and only you remained. Peacefully pristine, perfectly designed, from the labyrinth-like shrubbery pathways leading to the massive fountain with its towering goddess muse the mistress of this place was named after, to the wide open, tiered lawn taking up the full expanse of the back of the estate to a manicured woodland any fairy court could happily call its home, because everything about Vesterville's gorgeous landscape took my breath away.

All in no small part to the care and attention

taken by the owner of the whole kit and kaboodle. My daughter's girlfriend and the sole heir to the family fortune (thanks to her grandfather and some untimely deaths) might not have chosen the path she was on or the weight that was bearing the full mantel of the family name and fortune, but she took advantage of the sweeping estate's luscious landscape, her degree in botany a visible passion I wished Calliope would find a match to.

Though, as parked in the lovely lot created for visitors, a lot that hadn't existed a mere week ago, I reminded myself my daughter had found a match if one of love rather than career so far. That only added to the sense of calm and optimism as I exited my SUV and headed for the main showcase area.

Wouldn't you know, my girls decided to put on their very own flower show and horticultural fair, a grand event I'd at first worried might be a bit more than the two could handle, only to be proved wrong (of course I was, and happily) by the unfolding last-minute details I strolled past and through in the July afternoon sunshine.

My fight with Calliope back in April had never really been resolved, something that lingered like an ache I couldn't treat, that I did my best to stuff down despite knowing it only festered instead of healed. It was up to her to come to me, I knew. I couldn't address it directly, not without Calliope's permission, and she'd never given it. If I'd learned anything from her pushback, over her quitting school and so much more, it was that my daughter needed the space to find her own way and despite everything I tried to do (and not do to be a good Mom) wasn't helping.

I caught a short, hurt sigh and smothered it, my sandals stumbling over the edge of the parking lot's barrier of mulch and flowers, distracted thoughts doing nothing to help my situation. Too often I found myself returning to the hole inside, worrying against it like a sore tooth, fighting the need to confront her instead of letting her have what she needed to resolve it on her own.

Tough call, even for me. I only wanted what was best for my kid, but it turned out we had differing opinions on how I could deliver support. Still hurt deeply my therapist side came through more than the mom I wanted to be for her, and I felt my throat thicken with emotion despite the lovely day and the event grounds I now entered.

Calliope's stubborn refusal to discuss any of it with her father, FBI Special Agent In Charge

Trent Garret (since he was the only reason we knew she'd exited her business program early despite a full-ride scholarship) should have made me feel better, but it didn't. The fact he'd been spying on her behind her back, just like always (something about being a profiler and in law enforcement paired to his sense of over protectiveness made it impossible, it seemed, for him to give her the privacy she deserved) wasn't helping their relationship any.

Which only made me feel worse, ultimately. She'd made it very clear to me that my therapist Mom efforts weren't all that welcome either and despite everything I'd thought I'd done to let her make her own choices, to give her the freedom to be herself and find her way while encouraging her in whatever it was she wanted to do (or thought I had), Calliope's coming out as Thalia's partner had, according to said partner, given my daughter the liberation she felt she never had to speak her mind against her father's overbearing control and, sadly, my failed attempts to be the mother I thought she needed.

I fought off the kick of sadness, waving to Lloyd Mitchem, the estate butler, who hurried by with a salute of his own, the normally house-bound head of estate management pale in the summer's sunlight. It was all hands on deck if the dear older gentleman (forget he was a CIA agent once upon a time and could probably kill me with his bare hands if he wanted) was out of the house and hustling out here.

Thalia's excitement over the event she'd decided to host started only a month ago, gave both of my darling girls something to focus on, eased the tension between Calliope and myself, to my surprise and delight. Maybe it was direction she sought, not just making her own way. A route to follow, a goal to pursue. I was honestly amazed at how Thalia and Calliope, with the Vesterville's head gardener, Sandra Lin, as the official organizer, had transformed the rather stately side lawn (when I say lawn, I mean field, you know that, right?) into a terraformed overflow of flowers bordering new pathways paved in multi-colored stones, a massive stage set up with the backdrop of the estate house framed perfectly behind it, a giant greenhouse towering next to it, two stories of faintly tinted glass shimmering in the heat, both ends open wide to the breeze that would hopefully keep guests from sweltering in the damp interior.

I knew little about plants, to be honest, relying on my own hired gardener who came and pruned bushes, created flower beds, had his son run the giant lawn mower over my grass once a week. Not that I had a black thumb or anything or didn't like flowers and green things. I just didn't have the affinity for it. Thalia clearly did and I found myself smiling as I approached the merchant area, neatly set up tents in a small street of vendors offering landscaping, merchandise and information on everything to do with things that grew.

I was happy I made it before the official opening tonight at 6PM, wanting a chance to get a look around before the general audience arrived. My offers to volunteer assistance had been firmly turned down and I backed off, relenting graciously when Calliope again put her foot down. She'd never know how much that hurt me because I'd never tell her, and while I would have loved to assist, giving her the space she wanted and clearly needed had to be my priority.

Not that they needed me anyway. Sniff.

Okay, fine, enough with the silly self-pity, Persephone Pringle. Time to see what your girls made and tell them how awesome they were.

Speak of the pair, I caught sight of them talking with Sandra, their heads together, and approached with caution, though the moment Calliope looked up and saw me she beamed the kind of smile I remembered and adored and had to fight off a wave of tears that stung my eyes and tightened my throat. I hugged her instantly, her short, athletic body more her father than me neatly dressed in a white golf shirt with the Vesterville logo embroidered over the heart and dark blue dress pants, a clipboard getting in the way a moment before she flung her arms around me, pressing her curls against my cheek.

"Mom," she breathed in my ear, "how fun is this?"

I laughed, grateful as always for her enthusiasm, kissing her before letting her go, hugging Thalia, shaking Sandra's hand. The lovely woman who'd become Thalia's right hand in the estate's grooming smiled back, though I could sense the tension in her through her handshake.

"Nice to see you, Persephone," Sandra said, large, dark eyes that gorgeous almond shape I adored, her straight, black hair tucked into a neat ponytail, her own slim body dressed the same as Calliope, the uniform of her position making her look almost like a child, Asian heritage and delicate bone structure in full evidence. But there was nothing fragile about the way she turned to Thalia, hands on hips, nodding to Calliope.

"You have your marching orders," she said

in a firm alto. "Let's make this the most amazing show New England has seen in a decade."

Calliope saluted with a giant grin, Thalia laughing herself, the pale, tall blonde mistress of the estate's willowy appearance that underfed look of a high metabolism at twenty-two. Sandra headed off with a nod to me, Calliope in her wake, while Thalia lingered with me, holding my hand, her lovely white sundress dress covered in flowers, a fitting choice for the fabric considering. She retrieved a floppy hat from the grass and settled it over her pale hair, nose already red from the sun.

"She's loving it," Thalia said to me, glowing with happiness. A far cry from the young woman who asked for my help not so long ago, her family's fortune a giant weight on her shoulders. "Calliope's been shadowing Sandra and the two of them are the reason this is going to be amazing." She spread her arms, twirling a little, taking in what they had made. "Sandra was so worried when I asked her to create this event. She hasn't done one in five years. But when the chance came up, I had to take it."

"It's fabulous, Thalia," I said. "I know you don't need help, but if anything comes around, I'm here."

She stopped, face falling, staring at me with

those pale, blue eyes, before hugging me tight, the brim of her hat brushing against my blonde pixie cut.

"We'll always need you," she whispered. "Callie's being ridiculous." When she pulled away, her cheeks were pink, and it had nothing to do with the warmth of the day. Her gaze dropped before Thalia's smile flashed back into place. "I have a few things to do," she said. "Why don't you go check out the pride of the event?" She pointed to the greenhouse. "When I'm done, I'll come find you and give you a full tour."

I let her go, heart heavy despite my own smile as she left. Realizing I needed to mend whatever chasm remained between myself and my daughter. Because it was clear to me that Thalia's lingering hurt over our conflict was like the canary in the coal mine of our relationship. While I knew Calliope didn't want my therapist self, she was going to get her, and we were going to work together to fix what had been unwittingly broken if it killed us.

Excellent attitude, right?

Mind made up, I headed for the tall, glass building with hope growing alongside the gorgeous flowers.

CHAPTER TWO

You know those breathtaking moments when you stumble on something so utterly stunning and beautiful and overwhelming you can barely comprehend what it is you're looking at? That was me the moment I passed through the entry of the greenhouse and had my first real look at the contents.

The grounds, as I previously said, had been transformed into a wonderland of stunning detail, but this place took that to the next level and beyond. Maybe it was the initial inhale of deliciousness that had me gasping. Or perhaps the tiered displays, all packed with massive terracotta flowerpots, overflowing stations of three and four-level circular stands climbing toward the glass ceiling, bursting with color and life. The plethora of unusual scents and visuals took a long moment of *oh wow* to absorb, flowers I'd never seen before, depth of greens and golds and reds mixed with a rainbow of hues that had me stop, spiraling upward in kaleidoscopes of velvet petals and every shade of green. I'd been expecting something extraordinary, of course. But this whole vista stunned and almost overwhelmed via the delicious smells and mesmerizing designs that felt like an intentionally physical experience.

It took me a long time (how long I had no idea, really) to move forward, the overall greenhouse influence fading a little as I looked up through the tinted glass to the sun overhead, drawing in breath after breath of that most delightful combination of fresh soil mixed with exotic and truly delightful aromas, the mix of which changed as I moved through and around the displays of flowers. Not only did the experience change visually, but physiologically, the moisture in the air giving way at times to soft breezes that eddied around me, all while the scents mixed and mingled and shifted so naturally, I found myself lifting my head and letting my nose lead me, my vision battling for supremacy and tugging me in every direction.

I'd never been so engulfed by something

before and felt a giggle building, letting myself fall deeper into the experience. Every area, it seemed, offered a different combination of sights and smells, depending on the dominance of the plants being featured and I was hard-pressed by the time I reached the other end of the greenhouse (wait, how did I get there?) to choose my favorite.

Which meant I had to go back and start again, right? No argument from me.

As I made my way back, I took in further details, more man-made than grown. Like the placards of embossed gold on cream backers that marked each one, naming the designer and grower. I took my time on the return walk, trying to remember who created what, but quickly shaking my head at the effort. Over twenty displays filled the giant space with just enough room to circle each of the towers of blossoms without brushing against the bobbing flowers and leaves, the choices made by the creators blending colors and scents almost like oil paintings only better. Because these works of art were in constant motion thanks to the wide-open end doors of the greenhouse, what would most likely be overpowering humidity reduced to a tropical sensation that had me thinking I was on another world.

Okay, enough of the gushing, but honestly. So incredible. I'd never seen or encountered or experienced anything so beautiful in my entire life and for the first time, I understood Thalia's fascination with plants. Maybe I should take more interest in my own landscaping at some point, though for now, I was content to simply enjoy the contents of this stunning place and let the soothing stroll through what amounted to plant paradise engulf me.

"Watch out!" I spun just in time, a large pot tipping sideways nearly clipping me. Instinct took over, both hands catching the lip of the heavy terracotta, a young woman scrambling toward me to help support the other side. Together we managed to right it, the plants inside swaying as it settled on the angle originally set. "I knew there was too much weight forward," she muttered, digging into the soil around the plants before glancing at me with a faint frown and then realization and embarrassment took over. She whipped off one glove, sticking her hand out to me, round cheeks covered in freckles as was her nose, the light auburn of her wavy hair tucked under a ball cap, heavy ponytail swinging behind her over the shoulder of her dirty green golf shirt. "Sorry about that. Thanks for the help! Tansy Powers, Powers Flowers." She wrinkled her nose, laughed. "I know, I know. I've heard all the jokes, but my grandmother loves it so Powers Flowers it is."

I laughed at her rapid-fire chatter. "I love it, too," I said. "Your grandmother's a smart cookie. Persephone Pringle."

"Nice to meet you." She slipped her heavy leather glove back on, beat up enough I knew she had to be the real deal, her deft and concise movements as she reached into the tilted pot and adjusted the weight carrying on while she continued to speak in that fast, clipped accent that had to be from Boston. "I got here late. It's been a mad rush to set up. I should have brought an assistant. I don't know what I was thinking. There! That should balance it." She stepped back, exhaling a large breath before flashing me a smile, wiping at her cheek with the back of one glove, leaving a streak of dirt behind. She reminded me so much of Calliope's enthusiasm I laughed and didn't mention the residue left behind. She bore it like a badge of honor anyway.

"If you need help, I'm sure Sandra or Callie can get you some," I said.

Her hazel eyes widened, mouth falling into an O. "I'd never ask," she said. "My fault. Besides, having someone like Sandra Lin digging in my pots?" She faked a shiver. "I'd be terrified she'd judge me the whole time instead of on Sunday." She looked up at the plant taking up the top of the display, her expression shifting to nervous anxiety a moment.

Which had me staring, too. The lovely thing was truly incredible, the gaping lips of the flowers displaying a rainbow-tinted twist from interior to exterior, something I'd never seen before. Mesmerizing really, how the spiraling combination of brilliant tones covered the full spectrum from the tight base and waving stamen flowing outward to a soft completion at the outer edge. Thick, green leaves hung heavy around them, reminding me again of a painting, a work of art carefully crafted by the hands of a master (or mistress, in this case) instead of a plant. "It's stunning," I said, unable to come up with more despite wanting to. I honestly didn't know what else to say.

"Rainbow hibiscus," she said. Then, "I hope so," in a whisper. When she shrugged, there was so much anger in it, surprisingly. "I'm counting on the judges agreeing with you, Persephone." Her eyes narrowed somewhat, jaw setting, hands on her hips. Hard not to imagine a warrior going into battle. But it was just a flower, right? Not to Tansy, it appeared. "I have big plans for that plant."

"I've never seen anything like it before," I

said. "Did you create it yourself?" I knew enough to make that guess, figuring she'd forgive my ignorance and fill in the gaps.

I was right. People who create loved to talk about their creations and Tansy Powers was no exception. She nodded, though with less bubbling joy than I expected, more clinical as she went on. "Many of the plants in the greenhouse are hybrids, spliced purposefully by each creator to hopefully come up with a new and unique combination."

"Is there a lot of demand for it?" I had no clue really. Should have done some homework, apparently. But Tansy didn't seem to mind filling me in, moving to her next tilted pot to adjust it while we talked. Her speed speech had slowed somewhat, her Massachusetts accent as strong as ever, though.

"You'd be surprised," she said. "I'm really just getting started, but my grandmother, Lydia, has been growing and making hybrids for ages. She couldn't make it today so it's my first solo show." She hit me up with that sunny smile again, the faint gap between her front teeth adorable. "I just want her to be proud of me."

I was about to assure her that was likely the case when an elderly woman, her tightly curled white hair in a short and over-styled blowout framing her tanned and wrinkled face in a halo of glow, stopped and gave Tansy's stand the once over.

"Less pride and more luck," she sniffed, pale green eyes skimming the display, her thin lips pulled tight in distaste, lined hands and fingers curved slightly with what had to be arthritis brushing over the leaves and blossoms of the nearest flowers with a delicate and knowing but faintly trembling touch. Tansy's eyes flew wide at the gesture and Pearl quickly dropped her hand. Some kind of *faux pas*? Had to be. Maybe touching the plants was off-limits? I'd have to be more careful. The old woman's face settled into dislike as she went on. "Lydia's wins were never about skill, my dear."

Tansy blanched before her freckled cheeks bloomed themselves bright red and furious, blotchy marks appearing down her neck even through her tan. It was clear to me the attack was an effort to cover for the slip of fingers, but Tansy didn't see it that way and I hardly blamed her. "Whatever you say, Ms. Tolliver," she said, rigid now, her own hands shaking while she rearranged the pot, not so confident, her smooth motions choppy and nervous.

My motherly protectiveness might not have been welcome in Calliope's new existence, but that didn't mean it just went away. I turned with a fixed smile to the old woman in the blue dress, her hands now sliding into the pockets of her white cardigan, long, sharp nose turned up at the display.

"Persephone Pringle," I said, offering my hand. She shook it after a moment. "And you are?"

She seemed offended by the question, tucking her sweater around her despite the fact it was humid and warm in the greenhouse, her stick-thin body clearly struggling to maintain temperature. "Pearl Tolliver," she said. Waited in expectation of something. Recognition, perhaps? Likely, since the young woman next to me finally put me out of my moment of silent waiting for the other to carry on and explain further.

"One of the judges," Tansy whispered to me.

"A shame Lydia couldn't make it," Pearl said, raising her voice, circling past me to continue her disdainful observation of Tansy's flowers. Taunting her on purpose, it felt like. "I did so hope to dash her dreams again by calling out whatever you think that is." She jabbed an index finger at the rainbow hibiscus on the top of the display, her hand moving in the same slight tremor. "Lydia was only ever a fraud who stumbled on success."

"My grandmother," Tansy said through clenched teeth, "created more rare hybrids than anyone of her generation."

"Ah, yes, her claims said so," Pearl responded while I held off cutting in. It was obvious she was enjoying her cruelty but as long as Tansy kept giving back, I needed to stay out of it, right? Yeah, we'd see how much longer that lasted. "Except every single one of her so-called unique plants ended up being not so one-of-a-kind, didn't they?"

"Her work was stolen, and you know it, Ms. Tolliver." Okay, now Tansy was shaking for real and her anger reaching the point I worried she might lash out at the old lady. I stepped between them, my professional and inauthentic smile firmly in place.

"Perhaps there are other displays and creators you need to check out, Pearl?" I gestured to the next one down the line. "We should let Tansy finish her display before the judging actually begins." Did she get the hint that her choice to do so a day and a half early wasn't really fair? Not that fair was in this woman's lexicon. I worried about Tansy's chances with someone like Pearl Tolliver giving her grief.

Instead, she ignored my suggestion and

shrugged at Tansy. "I've known your fraud of a grandmother most of my life," she snapped. "If she ever made a unique hybrid, I never saw one. Talk is cheap, my dear, and so are Lydia's creations." She glared at the plant at the top of the display. "We'll just see how special your own so-called one-of-a-kind is when I get my hands on it."

If she got the chance. Might never happen if I had anything to say about it. Because if she didn't shut up soon? It wouldn't be the plant being manhandled, would it? Yes, she was an old lady. So what? Didn't give her carte blanche to be rude and cruel and intimidating just because she thought she could get away with it.

Tansy didn't get a chance to do much in retaliation, however, thankfully or not. And, neither did I because yes, I was Team Tansy and Team Powers Flowers and Go Lydia all the way myself and to heck with whoever this Pearl Whatshername thought she was.

Instead, with a waft of a powerful cologne that smothered the delicious scents around me in a miasma that had me flinching, I turned to find a tall, broad-shouldered man in a cream linen suit, his handsome face fixed in his own smile that didn't reach his brown eyes looming over me.

"Lydia's granddaughter," he said with

amusement in his voice and not a shred of compassion. "How charming."

CHAPTER THREE

Okay, now I had two butts to kick and felt less guilty about wanting to give him the heave-ho since he was over six feet and not a frail little old lady with a sharp tongue. Handsome or not, his rotten attitude instantly reduced his attractiveness from borderline model to rather distasteful. And that layer of cologne he carried around with him wasn't helping matters. One would think someone associated with flowers would want to be able to appreciate their scent, though it was quickly apparent someone like him had the kind of arrogance to think his own personal smell improved them somehow.

Yeah, failing, dude.

Tansy flinched back when he offered his hand, her nose twitching, so she was likely reacting to the scent as I was. But she shook regardless, either out of a need to be polite or a natural reaction to the gesture.

"Halliwell," Pearl said, lips twisting in further dislike, this time aimed at him.

He swept a cream fedora from his head, dark hair laced through the temples with silver. "Why, Pearl Tolliver," he said with a smirk. "How delightful. I hadn't expected to see you."

"I heard you were brought in last minute," Pearl sniffed, looking away, though perhaps she was accustomed to his cologne because her attitude seemed less grossed out and more disdainful. "They couldn't get anyone better?"

His perfect white teeth flashed on his tanned face. "Always a pleasure, Pearl." He gestured grandly to Tansy's display, brown eyes narrowing a little. "Halliwell Thicket, my dear."

"Tansy Powers," she said. Gestured at me. "This is Persephone Pringle." Nice of her to think of me, though more so I imagined a need for someone to have her back. Which I was more than willing to provide, accepting the request by interrupting before he could say anything further.

"I take it you're the other judge?" I knew Sandra was the third, but it wasn't hard to jump to the conclusion considering his conversation with Pearl.

"Indeed," he said, sweeping a bow toward

me, hat in hand. Seriously, how did he judge the scent of flowers like that? The man needed to back off the attempt to be his own blossom. "And, as Pearl indicated, a last-minute fill-in. Poor Theresa Umber had to pass, I'm afraid." His face creased into an attempt at sympathy that I read as underlying humor and delight. Nice guy. "Something about a sudden illness. And since I had a moment in my schedule between the product line launch and my new TV show filming, I decided to accept Sandra's offer to poke my nose into her little event."

And that was a leap into mean too far. Little event? He didn't know who he was insulting.

Pearl's scowl said what I wanted to, as did her next jab. "Some of us would rather take botany seriously," she said, "rather than turn it into a photo opportunity or a chance to peddle crap to amateurs."

And ouch. That landed visibly, Halliwell's fake smile flashing into a frown. "Some of us," he said, "aren't capable of more and will never do anything but judge others."

As much as I was honestly now enjoying the pair eviscerating one another, Tansy doing her best to not watch the impending train wreck while still trembling enough I knew she heard every word, it was time for these two to move on so my new young friend could regain her composure and finish her work.

"I'm sure you have better things to focus on?" I gestured at the displays around me. "And I believe you're here to judge the competition, not one another. Perhaps you'd like to finish your tour of the greenhouse?" Not really a question as I turned to Tansy and nodded with a pleasant smile. "The best of luck to you. I know you'll be a star." Then turned and firmly advanced on the others with my arms outstretched, both judges in my path, leaving them no choice in the narrow way between the displays but to move along now, nothing to see here, herding cats, thanks.

They wandered off, my ploy successful, while I paused one last moment to check on Tansy. She seemed to have regained her composure while I winked.

"That man stinks in so many ways," I said.

She burst into a laugh, pinching her nose. "Tell me about it." Then, she sighed, looking down at the pot in front of her, hands resting on the brim. "Maybe this is a terrible idea."

"No way," I said. "Your grandmother wouldn't have backed down and you're not going to, either. No matter what they say, you're here and that," I looked up at her prized plant, "is going to wow them and there's nothing they can do about it."

My little speech didn't land the way I'd hoped, her face crumpling a moment, but she finally rallied and nodded with a dimpled grin. "It'll all work out," she said, "no matter what happens. I'm doing this for Gran."

I waved and carried on myself, leaving the young woman to her work, hoping she hadn't taken the bullying to heart. It was clear to me the two judges weren't just cruel to other growers—the pair paused to pick apart a pair of women whose expressions clearly showed their displeasure at the encounter—but each other as well. Which led me to believe they were just miserable creatures who didn't deserve the power they'd been given.

That had me approaching Sandra with that concern in mind, the head gardener and event organizer already engaged in an argument with someone. She seemed much more worked up than he did, though as I neared, he shook his head and turned, exiting the conversation while she glared after him, hands fisted at her sides.

I stopped beside her near the entrance to the greenhouse, my need to express my worries corrupted by her unhappiness. "Everything okay?"

"Of course," she snapped before catching herself. "Sorry, Seph," she said. "I need to go." She hurried off then, through the greenhouse to the back exit, while I talked myself down from going after her. She knew what she was doing, and I had no clue about the ins and outs or goings-on in the botany world, right? For all I knew, the judges being asshats was part of the overall experience. I'd seen enough reality TV—baking shows, mostly—to know there was usually one judge with a bad attitude and a penchant for deprecation—maybe this wasn't unusual.

"I thought beautiful flowers were supposed to stay potted." I turned in surprise, the man Sandra had been arguing with now standing beside me. He was tall, like Halliwell, handsome, too, but there the resemblance ended. For one thing, that smile of his seemed real to me, one-day scruff laced with silver, his dark hair long enough to brush the collar of his white button-up. Blue eyes, open and sparkling with humor, caught mine, his crooked grin softening into a cough that bordered on embarrassment. "That was a terrible line, wasn't it?"

I couldn't help the laugh that escaped me, though thankfully it didn't come out as a harsh bray or end in a snort. Being single had its appeal, though I'd noticed, and not for the first time, I'd found myself feeling awkward around men now that I was divorced. Like being on the market again, whether I chose to date or not, flipped some kind of switch inside me that had my hormones reminding me I was only fifty.

"I've heard worse," I said.

That brought his grin back. "I'm sure you have," he said. "I doubt most men would know how to even talk to someone like you."

"Someone like me?" I arched an eyebrow, still smiling but now a little defensive. Had to work on that reaction, though it wasn't often an attractive man made an effort to flirt, so I wasn't arguing the experience, just his delivery.

"Unique," he said, gaze going to my blonde pixie cut, the tattoos on my shoulders and arms exposed by the tank I wore. "Likely independent and with little doubt remarkable. Intimidating, even."

Really? I wasn't sure what to say to that. So, instead of trying to flirt when I was truly terrible at it and he clearly practiced, I stuck my hand out instead. "Persephone Pringle."

He shook my hand with a firm but gentle touch, fingers lingering a moment longer than they needed to, though not in an unwelcome way. "Jason Arnold," he said. "What brings a lovely flower like you to an event like this, Persephone Pringle?"

"My daughter and her girlfriend," I said.

"Thalia has been part of my family since she was little."

"Ah!" He relaxed into our conversation somewhat, shoulders curving toward me, closing the distance without feeling creepy, creating instead a bubble of intimacy minus physical contact. "The adorable Calliope is your daughter?" I nodded. "You've done a wonderful job with her. She's as sweet as she is efficient." He chuckled. "I wish my boys were as motivated, but they seem to think living off their mother and me while they play video games and fail classes is their ideal."

My turn to laugh. "If only. My kid doesn't like to sit still. Gets it from her father."

"Not you?" Jason's head tilted, smile softening.

I shrugged at that. "I sit still for a living," I said. "I'm a therapist."

His blue eyes widened, but his interest didn't wane as I expected it to. Sometimes telling people—men, mostly—what I did for a living ended in a rapid retreat on their part. Kudos to him for holding his ground and, if anything, he seemed even more intrigued. "So, sitting still, for instance, over a dinner would be something you might consider?" Before I could respond, my throat closing over while my stomach did a butterfly dance of nerves I wasn't expecting, he gestured at my left hand. "That is if you not wearing a wedding ring isn't just something you and your husband agree to."

"Ex-husband," I said. "And I do enjoy sitting down to dinner." Did I just agree to a date? "That is," I repeated his suggestive words and tone, "if you like to sit down, too."

He nodded with a grin. "Not when I'm on assignment," he said. "I'm a reporter for the *New England Botanical Magazine.*" A journalist, how fascinating. "While I'm here covering the event I won't be sitting much. But after it's over…?"

I would have loved to carry on our conversation and find out just what that might mean, but an interruption had me jerking out of the intense focus I'd maintained on those truly beautiful eyes of his and to the man who huffed to a halt next to us.

"Jason." The intruder had no idea how close he came to me snarling at him to get lost. Held it together, barely. "Sorry to interrupt."

"Not at all." Jason gestured to me. "Have you met Persephone? Persephone Pringle, Darren Moorehead, manager of the East Coast division of PlantLife International." The giant horticultural conglomerate? Wow, that was a feather in Thalia's cap, having someone like that come to the show. "I was just complementing Persephone on the beautiful view." He winked at me while Darren smiled, shook my hand, though he seemed distracted.

"Very nice to meet you," he said before completely cutting me out by turning to Jason. "I'm not sure I'm comfortable talking to you about Sandra."

Wait, what? I kept my mouth shut, though Jason didn't flinch even though he had to know I wouldn't react well. Sandra worked for Thalia, and he knew very well how close I was to the trio who were running this event. Instead, he gave Darren an affable smile and spread his hands in a peace offering.

"I'm only wondering about her return to the event world," he said. "Considering her falling out with Halliwell five years ago and her departure from the circuit, it has to be a conflict he's ended up one of the judges."

Well, if what I'd discovered about Halliwell so far meant a thing, I was on Sandra's side in whatever battle they'd had. Would have been anyway, thanks.

Darren nodded. "I get that," he said. "But as a co-sponsor of the event, I don't think it's fair to undermine her. Not after everything that happened. I wanted to tell you I'm declining the interview before things get going."

"I understand completely," Jason said. "Have a great show, Darren."

Darren departed without another word, his phone clamped to his ear, not even a parting wave for either of us. I was about to confront Jason about his story choices and, yes, okay, dig into what he meant about Sandra and Halliwell, when he offered me a little bow and smile.

"I suppose I should get back to work myself," he said. "A true pleasure, Persephone. I'm sure I'll be seeing you again." He left before I could comment, watching him go with mixed feelings, observing his interactions with others for a moment to gauge his authenticity.

Was he really flirting or just being nice? So hard to know. While I was very good at judging the reactions of others in a professional capacity, it turned out I was terrible at gauging personal interactions. Besides, could I trust him if he was looking for ways to make Sandra look bad? On the other hand, maybe going out to dinner with him wasn't a terrible idea. At least for the experience. Surely, he'd be an entertaining dining companion and if I went into the date knowing I wasn't interested in anything aside from a meal, I might be able to see past the truth he was a reporter looking for dirt that might possibly influence Thalia's decision to have another show.

Did the fact I wasn't walking away outright make me a terrible mother?

Yes, yes it did. Then again, the girls were grownups, as my daughter so firmly told me. They could take care of themselves, right?

Hormones in a stir of *come hither*, I sighed and moved on.

CHAPTER FOUR

I paused near the entrance to the booths, taking note of a knot of people up ahead, two of them hardly a surprise when conflict was concerned but the third someone I felt protective of and so drew my attention. Though, it seemed Sandra was quite capable of holding her own against Halliwell and Pearl, perhaps because the other two weren't willing to put differences aside to team up against her. I didn't get to hear what it was they fought about, Sandra storming off, the tall and handsome judge going the other way, Pearl watching them with that pinched and hateful look before tilting her chin up and marching off herself.

Just as my kid huffed to a stop beside me with a huge grin on her face. "Mom, this is so exciting," she said, her enthusiasm cutting through my anxiety a little. "Have you seen Sandra?"

I nodded, pointed her in the right direction. "There seems to be a lot of conflict between the judges," I said before I could stop myself, wishing I'd kept my mouth shut.

Except Calliope didn't take it as an intrusion, snorting and eye-rolling. "Tell me about it," she said. "It's like trying to wrangle spoiled kids, Mom." She shook her head. "Thank goodness I never wanted to be a teacher and now I know why. I'd be terrible at it." She sighed, looked around with a huge smile. "But this? I think I might be good at this." Since the whole point of her leaving school was to find out what she wanted to do, I found myself discarding my concern about the judges in favor of stepping back and letting her have what she wanted without me poking my nose in.

"You're doing an amazing job," I said. "Have fun, honey. It's supposed to be fun."

She bobbed a nod, huge smile beaming at me, before she hustled off in search of Sandra and I took my Momness into firm control. Conflict was good for her, good for Thalia. From a therapist's point of view, learning to deal with such strife was a positive, not a negative, and despite her resistance to my psychological ways, I knew Calliope had the tools she needed to successfully navigate whatever crossed her path. Jason was right. I did do a good job and, to his credit, so did Trent.

Time to really step off, not just pretend I was, and let Calliope be Calliope without me standing behind her in the shadows with my hands out to catch her when and if she fell.

By the time I made it to the grandstand, the crowd of participants and visitors had filled the space, the staff welcoming them promptly at 5:30PM, event grand opening starting right on time at 6PM. I stood off to one side of the stage draped generously in gorgeous flowers, the arching blue arrangement behind the podium framed by the looming stone structure in the background. I did my best to ignore the weighty observation of Vesterville House, my lingering anxiety the place had a soul of its own that tied to the curse Thalia believed in at war with the fact I knew such a thing was impossible.

Until I stood in its shadow. Just a pile of rock or not, the place gave me the creeps.

I applauded along with the rest of the crowd as five people took to the stage, Thalia joining Darren on one side, Sandra, Halliwell and Pearl on the other, though it was Thalia who went to the podium first, her smile beaming out over all of us in the early evening sunshine.

"Thank you so much for attending the first annual Vesterville Flower Show," she said, followed by more applause. "Those of you who know me understand my deep love for all things botanical and I couldn't be prouder of what we've created here for your enjoyment." I clapped with everyone else. "But it wouldn't be possible without the support of PlantLife International and the experience of their East Coast manager, Darren Moorehead." He waved to the crowd but made no move to bump Thalia. "And my most enthusiastic thanks to the incomparable Sandra Lin for her efforts in making this all a reality. Her impeccable taste and decades of experience hosting and managing shows like this one, not to mention her incredible talent with plants, made the choice to make this event happen an easy one." Sandra nodded, smiling at Thalia. "We are truly honored to have Pearl Tolliver and Halliwell Thicket as our judges this year, both of whom will join Sandra on Sunday for the final determinations." Further applause and whispering. So, clearly, this crowd knew more insider information than I did, the ripple of gossip that followed Thalia's words making me curious now. "With that, I'd like to bring Sandra to the podium to talk more about the event." The clapping was polite enough as Thalia stepped aside and sat, Sandra taking her place with far less nervousness and a firm hand on either side of the stand.

"The official opening of the event is tonight," she said. "Join us for a cocktail party at 8PM in the gardens, mingle with the growers and merchants and enjoy yourselves." That seemed to meet with mixed emotion, though I personally looked forward to it. I guess not all flower people were social. "Tomorrow morning, the event opens at 9AM, with demonstrations here on the main stage as well as opportunities to shop with merchants at the booths," she gestured toward the little tent city, "and peruse the offerings our competitors have filled the greenhouse with." Again, not a flower person, so the idea of wandering around all day and talking plants didn't really appeal to me, support my kids or not. "Tomorrow night we'll be having a barbeque on the front lawn at 5PM, so please bring your families along if you choose." More lacking enthusiasm? These people did not know how to have a good time. "Judging will commence on Sunday," ah, there was the excitement, "at 10AM and the winners of each category will be announced at noon, right here." She stepped back, returning to her seat so abruptly it took a moment for the applause to start and even then, it came out awkward and sporadic while Thalia leaped to her feet and returned to the podium.

"We hope you enjoy your weekend with us," she said. "The Vesterville Flower Show is officially open!"

The final round of clapping ended quickly as the five on the stage exited, the crowd's exodus to carry on their own interests hardly a surprise. I thought about looking for Calliope and, instead, chose to leave her be, heading for my car and home to grab dinner and change for the cocktail party.

I'd hoped, as I dressed in the deep blue-green silk sheath I'd chosen for tonight, I'd have a date to bring with me instead of going solo. But my friend Lou Ellen Mallory was out of town on a hypnosis conference, so she wasn't an option. And Sheriff Cherise King, while it was Friday night and our usual dinner date, had gone to Portland with her husband and kids for the weekend. While I'd considered asking my mother to join me, it turned out she and her husband, Ralph, had already made plans to go hiking in New Hampshire.

And while, sure, I had other friends I could

have asked, I decided the Universe had another plan for me, that going solo was a good thing. Besides, as I observed myself in the mirror of my walk-in closet, the keto and extra weightlifting I'd been doing had whittled the twenty or so pounds I'd hoped to shed down to maybe ten, leaving me curvy enough I caught myself smiling at my reflection in the mirror.

Solo it was. Unless that handsome Jason Arnold decided I was story-worthy. Then, we'd see if I was on my own or not.

The drive back to the estate was a giggling nervous one while I firmly chastised myself for feeling like a sixteen-year-old hoping to catch the attention of her crush. I was a grown woman, for heaven's sake, had a grown woman daughter and a career I loved, was about as fiercely independent as Jason had imagined, unconventional, too. So, why then, as I exited the SUV, did I check my reflection in the black door to make sure I still looked good?

Vanity, thy name was Persephone Pringle.

Thank goodness for the platform sandals I'd opted to wear instead of the heels I'd considered. Sure, the cobblestone pathways might have looked pretty, but I felt a lot more secure with solid if tall shoes under me. I strode with confidence I wasn't sure I felt toward the garden and the sound of the party getting underway, smiling and nodding to a few people but not stopping, knowing I had a two-drink maximum and wanting to get a gin into me before encountering Jason again.

Not that I needed it, mind you. But a drink always relaxed me and besides, I had to drive later so better to drink now. Because yeah, that was the reason. Not the shudder of excitement in my stomach as those same traitor butterflies chose to do a dance of joy inside me.

The party area had been outlined with fairy lights and lattices covered in flowers and ivy, entrance flanked by two young men who waved me through, though I didn't recognize either of them. I scanned the thin crowd of people who'd arrived so far, noting I was probably the most dressed up and now feeling like a sore thumb waving a flag of desperation. *Notice Me!* The bar stood at the far end of the space so I bee-lined, weaving through the few folks who stood between me and gin, not noticing until I came to a stop with a little heave of relief I'd reached the bar without incident, I was far from alone at it.

The scent of his cologne was the first indicator, enough to cut through my anxiety and return me to reality, Halliwell leaning against the bar, watching the crowd through slitted eyes. He smiled at me, so of course, I smiled back because I wasn't rude. Had reason to be, of course, but couldn't muster it at the moment.

"You look like the kind of woman who likes a challenge," he said.

Oh, boy, another one? Only this time I wasn't interested in flirting. "Do I?" I gave the young bartender my order before turning to face Halliwell who held out his glass to me.

"Take a sip of that," he said, smile tight and expectant.

Did he know how creepy that was? Likely not, though I waved off his outstretched hand with a nose wrinkle and head shake.

"I'd prefer the bartender poured my drinks." The man had no idea how dangerous it could be to accept an offer like that one. No, I didn't think he was trying to dose me, but what kind of precedent would I be setting for my girls if I accepted when I'd counseled them many times on the dangers of drinking from unknown sources?

Halliwell seemed to have anticipated my reaction, likely because he'd encountered resistance before which only made him creepier. His expression shifted to cunning. "And here I thought you were brave. You wear a good game," he gestured to my dress, my tattoos, "but you're afraid of a little drink?"

"I'm incredibly brave," I said, "and brilliant enough not to accept a pre-poured beverage from a stranger."

We were gathering a little assembly, a few women observing from over their own glasses. Did they agree with me this guy clearly needed an education in how to approach someone without coming across as a total jerk?

That was my guess, but it certainly seemed Halliwell's offer had nothing to do with slipping me something I'd regret later and more about his arrogance, because he looked up and around and saluted the watchers with a giant smile.

"This is *Ascerbio*," he said, showing us the glass with the deep green liquid in it. "It's my favorite drink and I challenge any of you," he nodded to me, but carried on in that booming voice, "to take a taste without reacting." What was this?

"What do I get if I win?" Okay, he had me intrigued.

Halliwell shrugged, and I was positive he was going to say a date with him or something equally obnoxious. Instead, he pulled out his wallet and slapped a twenty on the counter. "Yours, if you succeed." His smirk told me he knew I'd lose.

Did I mention I might be a teensy bit competitive?

Oh, game on, bro. Game on.

CHAPTER FIVE

I took the glass against my previous better judgment, trusting that enough people watched if he did try to drug me or something equally hideous, I'd have lots of witnesses, at least. The rather slick-looking liquid had a bitter aroma, dark green tint a color I'd never seen in an alcohol before. Well, nothing ventured, right?

The moment the sip hit my tongue, I knew I'd lost because I could not for the life of me understand why anyone in their right mind would drink something so vile, so bitter, so revolting it made me gag before I could jerk the glass away from my mouth, barely resisting the urge to spit out what I had ingested—and it wasn't much—in the most unladylike fashion.

His mocking laughter? Just as bitter, the jerk. Halliwell took the glass back from me, holding it up, a lineup forming of eager tasters wanting to defeat the challenge no longer interesting to me. Sour and not just from his nasty concoction, I took my gin and cranberry from the bartender and swished a bit of it around to kill the disgusting taste in my mouth, only partially succeeding.

"I should have warned you," Jason Arnold appeared at my side, apologetic smile on his face though he glared at Halliwell who took a swig from his glass before allowing the young woman who was next to try it. "He's notorious for that trick."

"There's something wrong with his palate," I said, reminded of the taste as the girl did her best not to cringe, forced to turn away so nausea didn't win. "And him, in general."

Jason flashed me a grin. "You don't know the half of it."

"But you're going to tell me," I said, stirring my drink with the cocktail straw provided. "Is that it?"

His amusement seemed to fade a little. "I'm a reporter," he said, "not a gossip."

"I get that," I said, the hormonal reaction from earlier fading as I faced him down about what I'd previously witnessed. Grateful I had that to cling to and knowing it was likely a defense mechanism against the attraction I felt for him but unable or unwilling to stop myself. "You have a job to do. But I'm sure sharing what you know is a way to find out what I know because that's how it works, right?" I clinked the top of his beer bottle with my glass, grinning to soften the edges of my words. "I can tell you right now, Jason, I'm a terrible one to share with. I don't know a thing."

Jason didn't comment, glancing over my shoulder and, when his eyebrows shot up, I turned to find out what caught his attention. To find Pearl Tolliver, of all people, stood with Halliwell, his drink in her hand, her tentative sip sloshing slightly as her grip shifted, eliciting nothing but a shrug as she finished with a solid drink and handed it back before helping herself to his twenty.

While the crowd cheered, me included, an instinctual reaction. Halliwell's faint smile had me wondering, though he strode off with his empty glass in hand before I could sort out why he seemed so pleased. Pearl joined us at the bar, glancing at me before looking me up and down, reaching out to touch the hem of my dress.

"I love silk," she said. "What a pretty shade of blue."

Her attempt at being nice had me smiling in return, the shift in her attitude surprising. I almost corrected her, since it really was more green than blue, but the fairy lights probably had something to do with it and the detail didn't matter.

"That must have been fun to do to him," I said. "I don't know how you managed it."

Pearl smirked, tucking her cardigan around her, the pink dress she wore a little more tailored than the one from earlier but not much of an effort. "You spend enough time around plants, you learn to have a complex palate."

That was probably meant to be an insult, but again, I let it go because whatever, lady.

"You know Jason, of course?" I turned to include him in the conversation, finding him still there, waiting and attentive, though Pearl's snort and instant derision wasn't a surprise.

"Vulture," she snapped before marching off with her own drink in her hand while Jason waved at her as she went.

"Ah, Pearl," he said, "always a joy. But forgive me, Persephone," he said.

"Seph," I offered.

Jason's slow smile had that sexy edge that brought the butterflies to full attention, the brats. I took a long drink of my gin, wishing I didn't have a two-drink max suddenly when he nodded.

"Seph," he said. "You were talking about

sharing, I think. I tell you something and you tell me something in return?

I'd meant it completely differently than what he implied which made me giggle and wish I hadn't because it made me sound simpering and coy. Gross. While I despised the response, I was powerless to stop it.

Enter Calliope to the rescue, my daughter landing at my side like a tornado ready to take apart a small town. "*Mom*," she said, completely ignoring Jason as she hissed at me. "This party is *dismal*." She glanced around with her face contorting into frustration. "Can you please go do your thing and mingle and make people, you know. Laugh or something?"

"Hang on a second," I said, unable to stop the grin that crossed my face, "are you saying your mother is actually interesting and the life of the party?"

Calliope eye rolled with a giant sigh. "*Mom*," she said in that exact same tone. "They're *plant* people. They might as well collect *rocks*."

The laugh that got her had me caught between insulted and amused. "So, I can't go wrong, is that it?"

She tossed her hands. "You wanted to help, right? Stop flirting and get to work." She waved at Jason then hustled off while I leaned back against the bar and watched her go.

"I guess you're not the only one on duty," I said.

It was Jason's turn to touch his beer bottle to the lip of my glass. "Stop flirting, Seph," he said, "and go mingle."

I watched him leave, too, admiring the cut of his jib, you better believe it, the soft mellow of the gin hitting me just right, not enough to make me tipsy but plenty to relieve the last of my anxiety and kick up my happy.

I spent the next hour circulating as requested, cracking jokes that more than a few people found funny (imagine that), listening patiently to explanations of botanicals that made zero sense to me whatsoever, and doing my best to ensure Calliope's dismal party had a bit of life.

It helped that the crowd grew in numbers. By the time 9PM rolled around, I didn't have to work quite so hard, the chattering of the guests and their engagements increasing the noise level and the appearance that everyone was having a good time. Which meant, as far as I was concerned, my obligation was covered.

The only real irritation of the evening was the booming arrogance of Halliwell Thicket's voice. It had a penetrative power I wasn't expecting that only increased as the night went on, my second gin drained and water my new companion doing nothing to soothe the edges of that increasing grating tone compounded by the continual boasting he did at every turn.

Impossible to escape his endless talk about his new TV show, his product line, the drink he consumed in large quantities, over and over in a seemingly endless cycle that, despite where I stood and who I spoke to, managed to intrude in volume and content and annoyance until I'd finally had it.

Not that I planned to corner him and tell him he was a vain, loud blowhard no one liked and wished he would just leave already. Nope, I was a better person than that, heading out of the bar instead and into the garden proper. Only to find him ahead of me because clearly, I couldn't escape him, right? Watched him, his steps rather weaving and unsteady, as he crossed to the booth at the corner of the merchant aisle and circle the counter, taking note of the giant banner with his face on it, advertising his new show, *Plants That Kill*. Saw him pour a fresh drink from a bottle with a shaking hand, sloshing a little though it was clear from the way he shook out the last drops he'd come to the bottom. He then tucked the empty back under the counter before exiting in that same slightly staggering cadence.

Coming my way. Yikes.

He'd been out for a refill, huh? And too cheap to buy a drink at the bar, the tightwad, though he had said at least a million times tonight the alcohol that still made me wretch privately at the memory was all he'd drink.

I was a faithful gin girl myself, so I could understand the commitment. Just not the relationship. Yuck.

I ducked his return by hiding behind a shrub, not my best moment, made worse when I noticed Jason watching from the entry to the bar area. His laugh at my awkward escape wasn't helping any and while I was now free by my estimation to see what kind of badness I could get into continuing our conversation, there was no way at that point I was going to put myself in the position to be teased.

Which meant my night was probably over and that was definitely a very good thing.

One stop to make first, though I refused to use the portable bathrooms Thalia had installed for the event. Sure, she'd spared no expense, but they were still disgusting and since I had access, I chose to instead cross to the house and used the facilities there.

I was surprised to spot Halliwell again up ahead, staggering through the path into another part of the garden. He'd bypassed the party this time, clearly drunk and meandering, the fool. I scooted past where he wavered by a bunch of bushes, the sound of him divesting his stomach of whatever contents remained to it after all that alcohol consumption chasing me on my rapid way to the house.

Five minutes later, I hurried back down the path, ready to go home, hoping to avoid Halliwell and that he'd finished his own business and moved on. My focus on avoiding him meant I wasn't paying attention and, thanks to the fresh landscaping and tall bushes that made the side garden feel a bit like a maze, I ended up lost. Well, not exactly lost, but exiting in a different part of the event's layout than I expected. The back of the greenhouse had been closed up, doors shut for the evening, the sight of someone creeping toward them making me pause. When her head turned and Tansy's face caught the light, I frowned at her suspicious movements. She had every right to be here as far as I knew, so why did she look nervous?

None of my business and now that I had stopped, I realized just how much my feet hurt and that going home felt like the perfect ending to the night regardless of my ego's prod to go find Jason after all.

Which had me firmly marching down the length of the greenhouse toward the parking lot. I'm not ashamed to admit I meeped in fear when I almost ran into Darren Moorehead, the darkness in this area of the estate deeper than near the bar, the path itself lit but not enough to alert me until it was too late someone else was present. Not to mention the fact he came whipping around the corner at a clip and had to catch me to keep me from falling.

"Sorry," he said, glancing over his shoulder, then back to me. "Are you okay?"

I nodded, hand at my throat. "I'm fine," I said.

He hurried off without saying goodbye or another single word like he'd satisfied the requirements of apology and had his own life to live. Well, so did I, thank you very much.

When I turned to continue on, movement near the greenhouse door whipped my head around, the entry closing partway as whoever it was disappeared inside. I assumed it was Tansy again, though for some reason I hesitated.

You know how sometimes instinct takes over and curiosity wins despite the fact you could be the dumb cheerleader in the B movie who dies first? I didn't even know I was moving until I reached the door, peeking in around the partially opened entry. Darren had been hurrying away from something. What happened? And what was wrong with Tansy?

Yes, none of my business. I knew that, but the truth didn't seem to matter to my brain that moved my feet and pushed me through into the quiet and dark greenhouse without my consent.

Someone shifted up ahead, the silhouette pausing before running off while I frowned into the dark, hesitant at last, self-preservation kicking in. But my curiosity still had enough momentum I took another step inside, noting something sticking out past a display, only realizing what it was when I was almost on top of it.

Him, actually. The thing that caught my attention was one of Halliwell Thicket's shoes. The rest of him, it turned out, lay prone on the ground, his wide eyes staring upward, foam dripping from the corner of his mouth.

I didn't need the experience I already had with the dead to know he'd judged his last event and traded in for pushing up daisies.

CHAPTER SIX

I stood to one side, waiting my turn to spill the proverbial beans, as Sheriff Cherise King spoke with Thalia, her dark head down over the visibly shaking Vesterville. She'd arrived so quickly I was surprised to find her answering the initial 9-1-1 call, though her admission they'd ended up staying home came as a surprise.

"Layla was sick, last minute," Cherise had said like she believed her twenty-year-old, uh-huh. "No way were we leaving her home without supervision." Ah, so she tried the old *not feeling well, throw a party while Mom and Dad are away* trick? Yeah, that never worked out well. Good thing Cherise was smart enough to call her on it.

And not just so she wouldn't have to face a

giant mess when she got home. She had one right here that was all the complications she needed.

Calliope had already come and gone, hugging me tight, hugging Thalia for longer, but rushing off when the police cars arrived, flashing lights brightening the sky near the edge of the grounds where the event parking lot began. Hard not to stare into the hypnotic rhythm of the red and blue and white spinning, tempting lure a way to forget finding yet another corpse, because of course I did. Which meant I was likely the one that was cursed, not Thalia's estate, and for some reason death would now follow me everywhere for the rest of my own life.

Curses, huh? Yeah, okay. I was beginning to buy into the possibility despite myself.

I offered Owen Graves a wave, the young mortician/forensics expert/coroner (and who knew what else) for Wallace waving back, and I realized I couldn't remember the last time I'd seen him in normal clothes, the bulky white coverall and hood he wore far more familiar than it should have been, blue booties dangling from one pocket, matching gloves and plastic goggles in his right hand, the silver case of his trade in his left as he strode up the path toward the greenhouse and the body. The two EMTs trailed after him, carrying the gurney between them, waiting ambulance adding to the light show that we could have done without.

He paused next to me, offered a gentle squeeze to my arm before donning his gloves with snapping sounds. "Crap luck, Seph," he said. I simply nodded. "Anything you noticed that you think I should have a specific look at?"

I told him what I'd seen of the body, my attempt to feel for a pulse despite his obvious lack of breath or animation. Knowing touching the corpse meant my DNA would be present and wanting him aware of the fact. Not that Owen or Cherise would even suspect for a moment I was responsible, but I'd learned coming clean on every detail served me better than holding out and looking like an idiot—or like I was hiding something—later.

Didn't reassure me I was learning the ropes on how to handle a murder investigation.

Owen heard me out, gesturing for his EMT companions to carry on without him, then settled the elastic rim of his hood more closely around his face. "Thanks for that," he said. "I'll disregard your DNA." Owen hesitated a moment, turning a little pink. "By the way, is Calliope here?" He glanced around, swallowing in a way that made his Adam's apple jump. Then laughed a little. "Of course, she's here," he said. "Never mind."

"I'll let her know you're looking for her if you want?" What was this about, I wondered? Enough to do what I said I wasn't going to and poke my nose in. In my defense, he brought it up, didn't he? That meant I had free rein to at least clarify.

Oh, the endless sophistry I wove into a tight noose slung from my neck around parenting and curiosity. Hopefully, I could keep it from hanging me this time.

"It's not important." Owen said that a little hastily, in my opinion, with a hitch of nervousness and more than a little discomfort. His response did, however, mean my opening was cut off and it was time to zip it, Persephone. "I'll talk to her later. Thanks, Seph." He hurried off after the EMTs while I watched him go and pondered something that wasn't my business. As a distraction as much as anything, I swear, though yes, of course, I worried about my kid.

I might have agreed to back off and give her space but that didn't mean I gave up wanting her to be safe and happy.

A further distraction lured me away from that line of thinking when I spotted Sandra hurrying toward Thalia. On impulse, knowing Cherise would appreciate the time, I gestured for the gardener to join me. She did, though she seemed to do so with reluctance, slowing her pace, coming to a halt next to me with her gaze fixed on the young estate owner.

"She needs me," Sandra said.

"She's fine," I said. "Cherise is a friend." I touched the back of the head gardener's hand, drawing her attention. "Are you okay?"

Sandra frowned, nodded, the plain black dress she'd been wearing at the party hugging her so tight her waist looked impossibly thin. "I'm fine," she repeated the same sentiment I'd used. "This is horrible, of course. Will she shut down the event?" The fact that was Sandra's worry had me wondering.

"No love lost, I hear," I said. "You and Halliwell?"

The gardener shrugged, arms wrapping around herself. But Cherise and Thalia were heading our way, so she didn't respond, embracing the heiress instead before nodding to the sheriff while my insides did a little jealous jig of anger I squashed instantly. I didn't have a corner market on caring about the girls and being an ego queen about Sandra worrying for Thalia wasn't acceptable.

I instead focused on Cherise. "Sorry about this," I said.

She eyed me for a moment before sighing.

"Seph, if I thought it was your fault, I'd kick your behind myself." She shook her head, close-cropped curls shining in the turning lights from her car, dark skin such a contrast to the flash of her white teeth she almost looked like a shadow in the low illumination. "Tell me what happened, from the beginning."

I recounted everything I could think of, Cherise backing me up to the beginning of the night and the bottle of horrific whatever it was Halliwell had been drinking. She instantly sent one of her deputies in search of said bottle as I carried on, mentioning his staggering drunken session in the rose bushes where he and the contents of his stomach parted ways, but that was the last I'd seen of him.

A moment's hesitation later and I filled her in on what I'd seen, of Tansy sneaking around the back of the greenhouse, my encounter with Darren and following whoever it was into the space before they noticed me and ran.

"I couldn't see their face," I said. "It's too dark in there."

"Fair enough," she said. "Any of you know if he had a heart condition?"

Sandra instantly shook her head. Looked a little guilty, then tossed her hands. "We used to date," she said. "As far as I know he was perfectly healthy."

A deputy hurried up to Cherise, bottle in a plastic bag. I nodded to indicate that was the one I'd seen while the sheriff offered it up to Sandra for inspection.

"*Ascerbio*," she said. "It's all he'd drink." Yeah, got that much. Her face twisted in disgust. "I think he only drank it to mock other people. It's truly vile, about as bitter as anything I've ever tasted. Everything was a challenge to Halliwell. A war to be won." She sighed deeply, Thalia's arm going around her. "It's part of the reason we broke up."

But not the whole reason.

"Was he acting drunk all night?" Cherise focused on Sandra still, as if thinking the same thing.

She thought about it, staring at the empty bottle. "Not really, no more than usual. Though I do remember he mentioned he was feeling dizzy, having stomach issues." I didn't envy the deputy Cherise had sent to the rose bushes for a sample. "But he'd almost turned down the opportunity, said he was just getting over the flu. So, I thought he was being a diva." She winced. "Like usual."

The realization I avoided a dying man instead of checking in on him wasn't lost on me, nor was the guilt I'd made an assumption that could have cost him his life. No, I shouldn't have been feeling responsible. Still.

Do better, Persephone.

My part in the drama complete, I hugged Thalia, who clung to me a moment, voice low and sad.

"I told you this place is cursed." She met my eyes, her own full of tears.

What could I possibly say to that? Denying it wouldn't get through to her and might only upset her further. Instead, I touched her cheek with gentle fingertips. And made a decision I whispered to her. Saw her eyes brighten, felt with a lump in my throat the shaking gratitude in her next hug. Before she let me go.

"I'll be right back," I said. "Okay?"

She nodded, released my hand, head down, shoulders slumped. No way was I leaving things as they were, nor my girls all to themselves at a time like this.

And to be honest, I was in need of some company myself.

That's why I drove a bit too fast on my way to my own place, changing as soon as I got home. My fluffy white cat watched me from her perch on the bed, anticipating her attendance in whatever activity I had planned. Only watched as I bundled some things into an overnight bag and hefted it in one hand.

"Coming?"

She chirped agreement and followed me downstairs where I bent and hefted her against me (she'd gained weight since I'd taken her in) and carried my cat out to the car. Belladonna settled in her passenger's seat carrier while I drove right back to the estate, a faint sense of panic not lifting until I pulled into the parking lot again.

The police cars were gone, ambulance, too, the party over and gates to the event grounds locked up. That was fine since the main house was my destination. A press of the button at the entry and the massive iron gates parted for me to drive through, winding way to Vesterville House becoming familiar if not comfortable.

Lloyd opened the door and let me in before I could even ring the bell, my fluffy white kitty leaping down from my arms and sashaying of her own accord through the foyer. This wasn't her first time in the manor, so she knew where to go, light from the parlor luring her onward. I followed, bag over my shoulder, now wondering if intruding was a good idea, Thalia's openness to the idea meaning I was welcome as far as she was concerned or not. Only to find my girls huddled together on the sofa, both of whom squealed when Belladonna trotted into the room, leaping up on the pair of them like this was her house, thank you, and they'd better make room.

Calliope looked up while Thalia snuggled Belladonna, her hazel eyes sad. "Thanks, Mom," she said. Eyed my bag. "You're staying?" Was that hope in her voice? Did I make the right choice after all?

"Oh, yes, please, Seph." Thalia reiterated her welcome though she'd already told me as much, likely for Calliope's benefit as she handed Belladonna over to my daughter and rose, coming to hug me. "I'm so glad you're here."

I did it right. Imagine.

We didn't go to bed right away, though I could see how tired they both were, fought off a string of yawns, Thalia's anxiety improved but not going away until she finally came out and said what she feared.

"I thought I broke the curse," she said, Calliope making a soft noise of protest but her girlfriend carrying on anyway. "This family, the money, the house." She shook her head, blonde hair shimmering almost white in the light. "I wish I had never been born a Vesterville."

That ended our conversation on a note of dread, the tall, willowy girl who looked like a ghost to me, her pale pink dress from the party making all of her seem transparent when she left the room, head down, Calliope hurrying after her with Belladonna in her arms.

It was a restless night, I'll admit that much, tossing and turning despite the comfortable four-poster with its incredible curtained seclusion. Partly because I couldn't stop thinking about Thalia and the Vesterville curse and partly because I was alone. I'd become so accustomed to Belladonna's presence I hadn't realized how much comfort she brought me. Not that I begrudged the girls that same comfort, but the mix of anxiety after finding a body and talk of curses and the strange house with its odd sounds made sleep elusive.

The scent of bacon and coffee lured me downstairs, muzzy headed and yawning yet, to the dining room and the girls both already present. Belladonna perched on the table between them, princess cushion of her own providing access to the silver tray filled with a selection of what looked like fish and other tasty morsels I knew she'd adore.

"Don't get used to it," I said to the cat while the girls giggled. "You work for your breakfast in my house, missy."

Belladonna blinked at me before going back to her salmon.

Spoiled.

I'd barely kissed all three of them good morning when Sandra bustled in, taking a seat like she was expected. There was that jab of jealousy again. Of course, she was welcome, considering not only was she the event planner, after what happened last night surely, they had to have a strategy meeting of some kind.

"Have you heard from Cherise?" If she cleared them to go on, today could be interesting.

"She called just now," Sandra said, helping herself to some toast and berries. "She said to move ahead, that the team was done with the location. But she'll likely have more questions." The gardener seemed thrilled by that prospect.

Yes, sarcasm was my preferred weapon of choice when I was tired.

"We need a third judge," Sandra said. She met Thalia's eyes while the young woman's widened. "Are you up for it?"

That made her smile, turn pink. And I silently thanked Sandra for the suggestion if only for a moment of reprieve for the girl I adored.

"I don't—"

Calliope wasn't going to let her get away with that reticence. "Of course, you'll do it," she said with a huge smile. "You're the perfect choice."

Thalia's shy grin for her girlfriend ended in a firm nod for Sandra. "I'm in."

As happy as I was for the delight that gave her, why was I suddenly nervous Halliwell's fate might be linked to a threat to all the judges?

CHAPTER SEVEN

Breakfast wrapped up quickly after that, the girls scattering in their own directions while I lingered over my third cup of truly excellent coffee. The house itself might have been creepy, but the view out the dining room window into the lovely side garden had me smiling at the morning sunlight streaming in on the hardwood floor. I could almost imagine I'd made up all the spooky and oppressive things I'd thought about Vesterville house sitting there in a pool of warm illumination with the blue sky framed so perfectly.

The kind of day where awesome things could happen. As long as one looked past the corpse which, I realized, mirrored my thoughts about the estate house. If one could just squint and pretend death and destruction wasn't par for this particular course…

My phone rattled softly, the buzzing alert humming through the polished wood of the table. A quick check of my texts revealed a new message from Cherise that had me forgetting all about the happy possibilities the day could bring and slamming me right back down into reality.

Owen thinks it could be a heart attack or stroke, she sent. *But we're running a tox panel because.* That made sense. *Keep an eye out if you would. If you find out anything, let me know. I'll message you if tox comes back with suspicious results.*

Fair enough. And presented a modicum of relief, considering the last time she'd asked me to help her I'd skinned my knees on a few mistakes that had us at odds. Which meant two of the women I loved most in the world had their reasons to question my motives. Never sat well with me, apologies and attempts to rectify situations aside.

No matter. Cherise trusted me, even if my daughter still struggled, and that meant the world at the moment.

At least this time the girls let me help to my surprise and delight. Whether she realized the irony or not, Calliope herself assigned me to assist, my job to supervise the booths, making sure none of the merchants needed anything, guiding guests, and generally keeping an eye on things during this part of the event. I was more than happy to have the distraction, though the crappy night's sleep made me a little slow, nothing the endless supply of coffee the caterers kept us in didn't resolve for the time being.

It also gave me a chance to really observe Calliope in this new environment she was loving so much, proving to me once and for all her decision to leave school was the right one. Again, it wasn't that she'd quit that bothered me, only that she hadn't come out and told me, letting me find out when her nosy and protective father called the college when he suspected something was up. Still, I admit a part of myself worried about her choice since she'd been so close to graduation, only a few credits from her degree in business. However, if that wasn't what she wanted, why force her to carry on? Besides, I was sure if she decided to go ahead and finish in the years she had to wrap up said degree she'd do so exactly at the perfect time for her.

I really had done a good job raising her. Now I had to step back and let her know that.

Darren waved and smiled at me, his shift in attitude drawing me to him while he had a short break in customers. Word of the death had quickly spread through Wallace and whether Thalia and Sandra liked it or not, the lure of the tragedy had increased attendance well past what anyone had expected. So, I silently thanked Halliwell Thicket for his sacrifice as I slipped between two groups of shoppers and joined Darren behind the counter of his booth.

"Everything okay?" I smiled in return, the PlantLife manager shaking his head.

"Excellent," he said. "And a fantastic turnout. Listen, I wanted to apologize for last night." He cleared his throat, regret showing in his eyes. "I'd had a troubling call and I didn't mean to be so callous. Running into you like that."

My turn to shake my head. "All good," I said. "I'm sorry to hear that."

"And I'm sorry to hear what happened to you," he said, lowering his voice, one of his young assistants taking the counter when he stepped further back into the crowded booth. I joined him, wondering if this was voyeurism or something else. "It must have been horrible finding him like that. I should be asking if you're okay, not the other way around."

"Sadly," I said, "Halliwell wasn't my first corpse, so I assure you, I'm fine." I grimaced slightly. "Turns out I have this thing about finding dead bodies. I think I'm the only one who doesn't find it funny."

"That's not all either, is it?" I didn't notice Jason joining us, the reporter nodding pleasantly to Darren, forced to move very close to me, his chest brushing my shoulder, as one of the young assistants grabbed an item from a box and returned to the front. "You're also quite the master detective."

Darren's surprise had me laughing in denial.

"I do my best to leave the investigations to the professionals," I said. "But yes, I've been in uncomfortable positions accepting confession from those who've taken the law into their own hands."

"At gunpoint, is that right?" Jason whistled low. "I'm impressed, Seph. I knew you were remarkable, but I had no idea you were a superheroine."

He had to stop doing that or he was going to get himself kissed and I wouldn't be responsible for the outcome.

"The rumor is he had a heart attack." Darren didn't seem to be in a hurry to get back to work, letting the two he brought with him handle the bustling business, arms crossing over his golf shirt, slight paunch showing as he leaned back into the boxes.

"And I heard it might have been murder."

Jason's gaze fell on me, Darren's too until the uncomfortable silence thrummed as they waited for me to, what? Spill info I didn't have?

"The *sheriff*," I stressed her title, "will more than likely know if it was accident, natural causes or murder at some point. So, you might want to ask her." I tsked at both of them. "No sympathy for Halliwell, gentlemen?"

Darren grimaced while Jason shrugged. "Oh please," the rep said, voice still low but clearly happy to gossip regardless of what he'd told Jason previously, "no one liked the man. I'm surprised the TV producers even wanted to work with him or use him as a host. It's not like anyone in his personal life will miss him." He wiggled his eyebrows. "If he even had a personal life. As far as I know, he didn't have anyone to go home to."

"Not even Sandra?" Jason's soft question had Darren hesitating and reminded me of the conversation from yesterday. "I realize they aren't together anymore, but you don't think she would miss him? They had a past, after all. Love's an odd thing when grief is involved."

"You want dirt on Sandra," I turned to the reporter, fighting my annoyance and the continuing attraction I felt for him. "What did she do to make you target her?"

Jason seemed surprised by my wording like

he was about to protest. But it was Darren who answered despite the fact he'd told Jason he wasn't interested in an interview.

"You know they used to be a couple?" I nodded since Jason just brought it up again anyway. I wasn't stupid, grumble. "I heard he broke her heart, bad enough she left the circuit for five years. And," he glanced at Jason before going on as if he couldn't help himself, "not only stole her product line designs, the very ones he's been marketing," he pointed out the opening to a booth across the way, Halliwell's face advertising the TV show and his merch, "but muscled in on her production idea and convinced the producers to cast him as host instead of her."

Even more despicable than I thought. "But this is all rumor."

Both men exchanged a look then shrugged.

"He made a fool of her, make no mistake," Darren said. "And no one believed her when she tried to challenge him about the thefts. That means the product line tanks now, what a shame. And the TV show probably, too. Poor Sandra."

"Maybe," I said. "Or maybe Sandra will get everything owed to her now that he's dead."

Oh, Persephone. Why did you say that out loud? Though, from the thoughtful but hardly surprised expressions on both men's faces I wasn't the only one thinking it, was I?

Pearl Tolliver chose that moment to stroll by, the tiny old woman followed by what I could only describe as a pack of groupies who listened closely to her every word as she pontificated with hand gestures and great delight at the attention. She was so much more boisterous and charismatic than the woman I'd met yesterday I fixated and almost missed Thalia and Sandra following along, both of them appearing amused by the show they witnessed.

"That's another oddity," Darren said.

"Pearl?" I glanced at him, back to her. "She's clearly in her element. Maybe with Halliwell gone, she feels she can shine."

"No, not that," he said. "She disappeared for a year, no one heard from her. Stopped judging, stopped everything. Then, *poof*, out of the blue she's on the calendar again. This is her first show since last summer."

"She missed some of the biggest events of the year," Jason agreed, watching her with careful eyes, the reporter in him visible to me for the first time. What calculations went on behind that gaze I found so enticing? And was he trustworthy? "No one seems to know why she disappeared or what brought her back. I assumed she'd retired." He turned to me then, amusement gone, observant and intense almost more delicious than the sexy grin. "And Pearl's not talking."

"Sir?" One of the staff turned to Darren. "This customer has a question about the new product line." The kid sounded a little desperate, flustered, out of his depth. To his credit, Darren instantly sprang forward to help. Knowing he'd be tied up for a while thanks to the line now forming at the counter, I left without saying goodbye, Jason at my side, the warm sunshine a sudden shift from the dim interior of the tent, making me blink and shade my gaze, wishing I'd remembered sunglasses or a hat.

"I'm not targeting anyone," Jason said, voice surprisingly soft. It was hard not to frown in response because that was exactly what it felt like. "I'm just doing my job." He surprised me, freeing a set of silver mirror aviators from the breast pocket of his striped button-up, opening them and sliding the arms over my ears, settling the pads on my nose. Which he booped very gently, then grinned like he knew he'd just gotten away with something I wouldn't have normally tolerated. "Sometimes that means asking tough questions about people. And getting responses that aren't always the ones you expect. But I only ever report the truth." He leaned back, shrugged. "The curse of being a journalist is telling truths about people when they are connected to someone in particular you wish wouldn't be hurt or offended by what is uncovered." That was blatantly clear enough and made me blush a little. Hopefully, the heat of the day could explain my reaction away, but I had no doubt he caught it. "I like open minds, Seph," he said then. "There's nothing more attractive in a woman than an open mind." He turned nonchalantly, hands in his pockets, heading off to follow the judges, looking back at the last second. "I'm going to want those back." And was gone in the crowd.

I just bet he would. Growl.

Still not sure how to take him or his decidedly intimate and yet perfectly casual advances, I returned to the job, continuing my endless pacing of the booths when a flash of white at the end of the row dashed across the path of two women who cried out in surprise only to disappear under a shrub.

Which had me running panicked at full tilt, heart pounding, in pursuit of my escaped cat.

CHAPTER EIGHT

She ran from me, the bratski, dodging as I chased after her through the garden, streak of fluff enjoying her freedom a bit too much, evading me easily. The handful of people wandering the grounds did nothing to slow Belladonna's joyful gallop through the event site, moving so fast no one had time to stop her or even thought to.

It wasn't that I denied her outside activity or anything. My back yard was fully fenced, and she seemed content to lounge on the deck and explore my existing flowers and bushes, eating the occasional bug before I could stop her (gross) and generally enjoying the sunshine with me supervising.

This was a far different set of circumstances and, from the way she enthusiastically bounded in her effortless feline freedom, she knew it. This was no secluded and safe home retreat where she couldn't wander into traffic or be harmed by some unknown and unforeseeable event. Yes, I was imagining worst-case scenarios as I chased her, because she was a helpless kitty in a strange place and who knew what horrors awaited her if she escaped for good and never came home? I know, I know, I was likely overreacting as I panted and wished I'd been working on my cardio a little more while she seemed to have found a limitless supply of her own energy, always ahead, just in sight but no closer than she'd been before.

The logical part of me knew she'd be back after some exploring. She'd been a free-range and rather feral creature when I'd adopted her (who was I kidding? *She* adopted *me*) and knew her way around. Thing was, she hadn't been exposed to this kind of situation before. The fact the place was packed, and she was so friendly had me worried she might trust too much. Get snatched. Sigh, don't judge me. I loved Belladonna and the idea of her being catnapped, while utterly preposterous, crossed my mind a couple of times mixed in with the fear she might get hit by a car if she made it to the parking lot. Or stuck up a tree she couldn't maneuver properly. Encounter a stray wild animal bent on doing her harm.

The panicked disaster scenarios seemed to be never-ending. And, the truth was, the estate wasn't just vast, it bordered on a forest. Which meant if she did keep running, got lost, wandered somewhere she wasn't meant to go, I'd never see her again.

And I'd never forgive myself.

I don't know if you own a pet or have had these kinds of thoughts yourself when said furchild managed to escape into the wild unknown and give you heart failure over the possibilities of their demise and/or injury. Whether you've endured such a situation before or not, I found myself in the throes of agonized fear and frustration, mixed terror and anger at her continuing scamper out of reach, I was ready to murder her myself when I caught her because if she got herself hurt or harmed or—heaven forbid—killed, she'd wish she'd kept running.

I know I wasn't making sense. That was anxious hysteria for you.

I almost lost her, panting, swearing under my breath, my temper rising, when I emerged suddenly into a small courtyard-like area that led to a gate and a fence of hedges. A closed gate, no less, a fact my cat ignored, choosing the greenery as her hurdle. She leaped with an agility I wished I could mimic, flying white bundle of fur and rebellion, disappearing into the sheltered space beyond.

At least I had her cornered, right? Sure, I did. For all I knew she'd just find the other side of the space and hop it and leave me behind, laughing her cat laugh at me. Well, we'd see who had the last laugh when she ran into trouble, and I wasn't there to save her furry behind.

Of course, I carried on after her, though, as I passed through the gate, I had a moment of concern at the small sign mounted on it, one I hadn't seen before. I barely caught the DANGER warning, but that was all that I required, not stopping to inspect why I should be careful and what exact danger might be lurking, my previous fears now exponentially expanding to include instantaneous death without cause and supernatural encounters because this was, after all, Vesterville we were talking about.

My attempt to move fast in pursuit didn't work out the way I'd planned, forward motion stymied by the choice of paths on the other side of the gate. Did she go left? Right? Or down the middle? There was no sign of her straight ahead, so I took a chance after a groaning moment of concerned indecision and went left. Naturally, it was impossible to see more than six feet ahead. Where even was I? I didn't think I'd ever been in this particular part of the garden before, a small half-greenhouse dome partially open to the sky looming behind the circular patch of flowers and plants surrounded entirely by the shoulder-height shrubs my cat decided to play steeplechase over.

The path led in a curved turn around the hedge, a spiral, I realized, divided down the middle by a straight line she avoided because that would be too easy. It wasn't until I'd made it almost to the center of the seemingly endless vortex of plants and flowerbeds, that I almost stumbled over Belladonna. I came around a corner at a trot and found her sprawled out on the walkway, panting and clearly pleased with herself, pink tongue hanging out and full tail flicking in obvious enjoyment.

"So happy you're having fun," I snapped around my heavy breathing. "If you're done, I'd like to forget you scared the living daylights out of me, missy, and take you back to the house where you need to stay put."

She chirped at me, and though I knew she didn't speak English, I was positive she just told me where I could take my attitude and shove it.

I advanced on her, hoping she'd behave and hold still long enough for me to get my hands on her. But she'd clearly worn out her excess of energy, making no move to run away when I crouched next to her, hands stroking her fur, glancing sideways at the flower bed beside her.

Realizing she lay right next to a patch of plants where the soil had been so disturbed the roots of one of them showed, torn and damaged. Lovely, not just an escaped convict but a vandal. Then again, she may have been innocent, because her paws seemed only moderately dirty from the run, not caked in the kind of mess that would be necessary to create such a hole.

Knowing Thalia would instantly forgive her, I still hoped Belladonna was innocent of planticide. Not like she cared, but this section was closed off for a reason I still didn't understand and for all I knew, these particular ones were valuable and important. Leave it to my naughty cat to ruin something that maybe took ten years to grow or cost a million dollars or once belonged to the Queen of England or something.

I pivoted to check the damage further, happy she was okay and yet trembling regardless, the adrenaline wearing off and leaving me tired and sweaty. She meant a lot to me, the careless creature, whether she knew it or not. "What were you thinking?"

She chirped a casual meow of *none of your business* and began grooming one paw, pausing to pant a little more. I considered fixing the mess she may or may not have made and decided against it. Not only was honesty the best policy but I'd likely do more harm than good. Instead, I sat next to her, stroked her fur. "I know your first year was spent wandering," I said. "You had the whole beach and everything to yourself." She didn't comment, tail flicking. "But this isn't Zephyr, Bella. Wallace is a big town with cars and wild animals and a lot of people. It's too dangerous for you to just run around on your own."

She meow-yawned and went back to cleaning, this time focusing on her face and right ear.

I frowned at the mess she'd made (jumping to that conclusion seemed logical at this point because blaming her felt like vindication for chasing her all that way only to find her perfectly fine and safe) and read the placard next to the purple flowers whose roots she'd so rudely exposed. "I have no idea what *aconitum napellus* is, young lady," I said, "but I highly doubt Thalia would appreciate you digging it up."

Belladonna's ears perked, the sound of footfalls the only warning I had, though she clearly knew well before me we were about to have company. Only to find Thalia and Sandra, Pearl and her entourage in tow, coming to a startled halt on the path.

Thalia's reaction was so violent I almost cried out, the young woman's horrified expression as she lunged for the cat and lifted her into her arms making me so anxious, I hugged them both.

"Seph, she can't be in here." Thalia pointed down at the plant, her eyes widening while Sandra crouched to look over the damage, the young heiress instantly checking Belladonna's paws before she exhaled in relief. "That's wolfsbane," she said. "Monkshood. Seph, it's deadly poison, all of the plants in this garden are."

I had Belladonna in my arms, checking her dirty but not digging dirty feet myself. "Why do you have something like this hanging around?" I didn't mean to sound accusatory, but my cat's safety was my priority.

Thalia looked around, sadness on her face, Pearl observing her with a pinched expression while Sandra straightened, frowning at the broken plant. "There are so few gardens like this one," she said. "I have scientists all over the world who request samples for study of the poisons and toxins they produce. And they are so beautiful. They deserve to live. It's not their fault they can kill."

Okay, I really needed to get this girl out of that creepy house before she turned into some kind of genteel poisoner. Except Sandra was nodding, arm around Thalia's shoulders.

"The cat didn't do it," Sandra said. "Looks like someone was messing around." Again with the frown.

"There's a sign at the gate," Pearl said then, interrupting. "Didn't you read it?"

Yeah, like my cat could read, lady. I didn't bother mentioning I'd failed to stop and scan it fully because it didn't matter now and informing her there wasn't time during the heat of the chase seemed like it might fall on deaf ears. Anyone who didn't put the safety of pets ahead of personal judgment had no place in my life, thank you. "I'll take Bella back to the house." And give the maid who was supposed to be watching her a talking to. A firm talking to.

Thalia hugged me tightly again, stroked Belladonna's fur while the cat purred in contentment, not a care in the world she'd almost given me heart failure. Two bodies in two days would be more than I was willing to tolerate, especially if one was mine.

It was a longer walk back than I expected, not realizing how far the cat had led me, but when I did finally reach the edge of the greenhouse and caught sight of the distraught and crying maid, I'd calmed enough I was the one soothing her instead of giving her trouble. I sent her off with the now lazy and tail-twitching Belladonna, the cat watching me over the girl's shoulder with those green eyes challenging me to keep her inside and now that she'd tasted freedom?

Not only was my daughter all about having things her own way, I had to adopt a cat with a similar MO.

I was so screwed.

CHAPTER NINE

I took time off that afternoon to watch some of the lectures, a bit bored by the time lunch was over with the job I'd been assigned. Pacing back and forth in merchant alley when no one needed anything, and the crowd vanished anyway once the sessions got started had me inclined to check out what the buzz was all about.

She might not have been my favorite person in the world at the moment (yes, I was still stinging over her callous comment about Belladonna, thank you), I did find it fascinating to listen to Pearl talk about her experience with perennials. The woman had been in the flower business since her childhood, decades of experience, anecdotes and advice that had her watchers laughing as well as writing notes assured me she at least knew what she was talking about. She might not have been the nicest person on the planet (sarcasm, my dear friend), but she certainly lit up when she talked about her favorite topic.

And, whether I liked her personally or not, I had to admit her enthusiastic and educational presentation had me yet again wondering if I could possibly learn to like gardening.

I knew better, of course, but that kind of articulated joy was hard to shake.

Sandra's discussion, while a bit more reserved, was no less informative. Her carefully laid out and clearly practiced talk about best plants for indoor, outdoor, water and specific light preferences only added to my wistful fantasies about long, flowing gowns and strolling at midnight through rose gardens while moonlight bathed my perfectly landscaped backyard in silver perfection.

Yeah, that was going to happen. Still, while not exactly overly excitable like Pearl had been, Sandra's precisely logical and incredibly fact-dense delivery wasn't helping matters. I had put my foot down at too much inside the house up until now. Not because I didn't want to water them (okay, I didn't want to water them and knew I wouldn't water them, and they'd die, and I'd feel guilty) but because I knew my bratty fluffchild catbratness would dig in the soil and make a mess as often as felinely possible.

Yeah, I prized my clean home (and clear conscience of not being a plant murderer) too much, thanks.

But it was Thalia's talk—meant to be Halliwell's, as it aptly turned out—that had everyone's rapt attention. I clapped with more enthusiasm than the crowd who'd come to listen, the thin gathering irritating when she was introduced. What was wrong with people that they weren't running to take a seat? Thalia cleared her throat at the microphone, smiling at me while she got started.

"I'm honored to be here today," she said. "And while my presentation might not have the same drama as the one originally planned," laughter at that, despite Halliwell's state of deadness, "I hope you enjoy what I have to show and tell you about the most remarkable of plant categories—those whose physiology create toxic and poisonous reactions in other living things."

She might have started out with only a dozen or so watchers, but her voice carried, and it only took a few minutes for others to join, for the seats to fill, and finally, for standing room only while I beamed in pride and knew I'd be hugging her later.

Thalia's introversion vanished as she unfolded her exhibition, Calliope joining her on stage with her own visible delight in her girlfriend's delivery showing, playing Thalia's assistant and bringing out for perusal different plants the Vesterville heir then explained in great detail and with enough theatrics I was laughing and applauding with the rest of the crowd.

She'd missed her calling, I realized, a life on stage something she'd have excelled at given the opportunity. Though, it was easy to see that it wasn't just the place she stood or the chance she'd taken but her love and adoration of the plants she shared that gave her the real glow she wore the entire time.

Plants That Kill became *Natural Plant Defenses*, but with no less impact. While I was sure the perished expert would have carried on in the most over-the-top fashion possible, Thalia's warm and enthusiastic talk, done with her delicate paleness backed by sunlight and that same ethereal feel of her I'd seen the night before even more apparent, she captivated with details about plants deadly to humans and animals alike, the more beautiful and poisonous the better.

She flushed when they applauded at the

end, cheered, really, Thalia's joy at the rapt audience making me grin so wide my cheeks ached.

"Isn't she amazing, Mom?" I didn't notice Calliope had come to stand next to me, that she'd circled around the crowd, her job now done, giving Thalia the stage to herself because she was an awesome and amazing creature and I'd done good with her. I just nodded, my daughter's love shining in her eyes when she turned back to watch Thalia take a giggling bow. "She's the star of the show and she doesn't even know it."

I hugged her around the shoulders. "That makes two of you," I said. "She couldn't do this without you."

Calliope shrugged but didn't deny the compliment. "We fit really well," she said. "I can't believe we waited this long to…" she stopped, chin dropping. "I love her so much, Mom."

"I know, sweetheart," I said. "And that makes me very happy."

She sniffled, turned away, but not before I saw a tear fall from her cheek. By the time she reached Thalia she was all beaming smiles again, her girlfriend hugging her tight, the two lost to the rest of the crowd as they kissed briefly, Thalia shyly, Calliope with exuberance.

Young love. Sigh.

The moment of celebration wasn't meant to last, however, Tansy Powers storming into the education space, her face red, whole body shaking. And spoke before I could grab her and find out what was wrong.

"I've been robbed!" Everyone turned toward her while she burst into tears. "My hybrid's been stolen!"

I comforted Tansy, or did my best to, arm around her while Thalia handed her a glass of water, Sandra in the huddle, Calliope gone running off somewhere, more than likely to confirm the theft. The young woman shook, barely able to sip the cold liquid, still weeping, in shock. And as selfish as the thought was, I'd hoped to at least preserve a few minutes of privacy, not to deceive anyone but to take the time to figure out what happened before word got around. After all, if the thief thought they'd gotten away with their act they might be less careful and easier to catch.

Not a likelihood, but at least a possibility.

Yeah, that went out the window with Tansy's continuing rant from the moment she revealed the disaster. If the house staff didn't know I'd be surprised. There was no way to keep it quiet, not now, Tansy's outburst meaning the second disaster of the event weighed heavily, not just on the owner of the alleged stolen flower, but on the young woman I adored. I was surprised, however, at Thalia's composure, how she moved with surety and unshaken focus. As for her compassion, well, that came as no surprise at all. Even at her most pressured the lovely blonde willow put other people's hardships ahead of her own.

Meanwhile, Tansy fretted and spluttered and struggled to regain her composure, overdoing it a bit, if I was going to be honest, though I really had no idea what was actually at stake so judging her wasn't helping matters. Still, it was a flower, for pity's sake. Just a flower. It wasn't like someone killed her.

Oh, Persephone. That was beneath you.

"It's not fair!" Tansy wailed that statement, catching the attention of a passing group who whispered among themselves after the fact. I'd tried to guide her, yet again, away from the main area, but her resistance continued, meaning she ended up sitting on the counter of the unused Halliwell Thicket booth, right in the path of everything. No irony there, his smiling face beaming down on us, her choice of perches a reminder of what happened last night and only adding tension to what unfolded now.

No, I was not thinking about the Vesterville curse. But you better believe Thalia was.

Trying to move Tansy at this point made no sense, so I simply supported her and hoped she'd calm down, something I was pretty sure lay in the far distant future. "My grandmother's creations were all stolen and now mine has been, too. Someone's targeting me, I know it!"

Sandra didn't deny it, a fact that had me frowning. "I'm so sorry, Tansy," she said. "We'll get to the bottom of it."

"You won't." The girl shoved away from me, weeping again. "You won't because no one ever does. No one wants to admit that plants get stolen all the time, that the real owners and creators are cheated out of their hard work. No one talks about it and I'm sick of it!" She stormed off, Thalia about to go after her when I caught her arm.

"Is she right?" Thalia shrugged but Sandra was nodding, grim, sad.

"Unfortunately, it does happen," she said. "But I never expected it would here. Not with the newness of the event." She winced, apologetic expression aimed at her boss. "We just didn't attract enough stars to lure a thief. At least, I didn't think we had."

I caught sight of Cherise approaching waving for me to join her, so I left Sandra and Thalia to deal with Tansy as they chose, slipping between two booths to the back of the area where the sheriff let out a long breath of air, fanning herself.

"How did you know Tansy's plant was stolen?" Did someone call her?

Cherise frowned, shook her head. "Whose plant?"

Of course, she wasn't here for that. "You got the tox panel back." The fact she was here in person didn't bode well.

The sheriff nodded heavily. "I'm afraid so," she said. "Halliwell Thicket was poisoned, Seph. By the drink he brought with him. Some kind of plant toxin, the lab said."

And I suddenly had a terrible, terrible feeling as my mind flashed to Belladonna and the purple flower with the dug-up soil, the damaged roots. Thanks to Thalia's class, I now knew that monkshood, wolfsbane, was not just deadly, it was one of the deadliest plants in the world, from the lovely flowers it produced to the leaves, stems and yes, even those white roots.

"Let me guess," I said. "*Aconitum napellus.*"

That frown of hers deepened, her head bowing toward me, broad shoulders squared as she planted both fists on her hips.

"Spill, Pringle," she snarled. "Now."

Didn't work out that way despite her demand, instead ending with me dragging her to where Thalia and Sandra now stood near the door to the greenhouse, looking up when I huffed to a halt.

"Tell them," I said to Cherise.

"What's *aconitum napellus*?" She met with two very shocked faces that paled out as they realized why she asked.

"It can't be," Thalia whispered, one hand over her mouth, turning to Sandra.

The gardener, for her part, nodded grimly. "Is that what killed him, sheriff?"

Cherise wasn't done scowling or with her fists-on-hips pose. "Someone tell me right now why this is the giant problem I'm now thinking was just a small one."

"Because I grow that plant on this estate," Thalia said, "and thanks to Belladonna and Seph, I was made aware that very plant had been disturbed since yesterday."

"You're telling me the poison that killed Halliwell Thicket wasn't imported by some plant person with a grudge," the sheriff said in a cool but clearly angry voice, "but by one you personally own and cultivate?"

"It causes paralysis of the heart," Sandra

said then, tone dull, eyes sad. "And respiratory system. Dizziness and vomiting are symptoms of poisoning."

"In other words," I said, "they can make the person who's been poisoned look drunk."

Sandra swallowed, looked away.

While I realized my mistake wasn't just that Halliwell needed help, was having a heart attack. He'd been poisoned, was dying all night and no one even realized.

Or cared.

Yikes.

CHAPTER TEN

I quickly spun on Thalia, panic in my chest though I knew already my fear was unfounded because I was fine, right? Except wait, maybe I wasn't feeling so well but that had to be psychosomatic, yes? Yes. Of course, it was. Calm the heck down, Persephone Pringle.

"I tried his drink." That came out clear at least, surprisingly. But what was it about near-hysteria despite logical alternatives that had me talking so *fast*? Like, spilling four words at lightning speed? Adrenaline, my dear. A giant hit of it and likely more to come, so pace yourself, girlfriend. "A lot of people did." I gasped then, my personal fears turning to a group poisoning of epidemic proportions. "Pearl." That tiny little old lady. "She drank a whole gulp." Which was what snapped me out of it, ultimately.

Because come on now. Here we were, walking, talking, breathing. Carrying on as if not poisoned or pending death at any given second, at least not from Halliwell Thicket's unfortunate drink of choice. Since I hadn't heard of (or, let's be honest, stumbled over, far more telling) any other corpses since his, it was highly unlikely anyone who drank from his glass suffered ill effects of their own.

A poison like that had to kill pretty quickly, didn't it? Of course, it did. Hysteric reactionism did *not* become me even a little bit. There was also the fact the experts, Thalia and Sandra, both rushed to reassure me.

"You would have felt something by now," the gardener said.

"Oh, Seph, it's so scary but I'm sure you're fine," Thalia spoke over top of her gardener. "But we can call a doctor and check, just in case."

Cherise instantly waved off talk of medical assistance, taking a minute before sighing.

"Again, my hopes his bottle was pre-tainted are dashed," she said. "In other words, if everyone else is fine," she gave me the stink eye of *keep it together, sister*, "the bottle was likely not poisoned until later in the evening."

Of course. That made total sense and I just

made a giant fool of myself panicking over nothing at all. Except he'd died so maybe not nothing. Hey, I really liked my life finally and I wasn't ready to give it up because some arrogant asshat who no one liked got himself poisoned because well, no one liked him.

Someone specific and for a purpose still unknown but more than likely tied to, you guessed it. *Not liking him.* Hate was a powerful motivator.

"It would take about an hour for it to slow his heart rate and respiratory system," Sandra said. "So, yes, that makes sense."

Phew. Like, giant phew. Wasn't ready to join Halliwell in the great beyond, thank you.

It did mean another walk to the deadly garden, to show Cherise the plant in question. She examined the soil, looking up at Sandra. "I don't see any damage here."

The gardener seemed at a loss, glancing at her boss then back to the sheriff. "I didn't think anything of it," she said. "So, I fixed it." Regret flashed over her face. "I'm sorry, sheriff, I swear if I'd known it was monkshood that killed Halliwell I wouldn't have touched the plant."

Cherise stood, nodding. "You realize how that looks, though, Sandra." Not an accusation, more a tired admission.

The gardener's mute stare answered her while Thalia quickly leaped to her defense.

"Sandra had no reason to hurt Halliwell Thicket," she insisted while my sad headshake silenced her, Cherise noting it, focusing on me, Sandra's continuing shock and horror keeping her silent.

"That's not exactly true," I said. "You were a couple, Sandra, about five years ago?" She met my eyes, pleading with me without saying a single word. "Is it true he broke your heart? Stole ideas from you, even the TV show you wanted to produce?" Sandra moaned ever so softly, a protest but not a denial.

"I already know about the lawsuit you dropped," Cherise said. She was already on it, good to know. And a relief I wasn't just spreading gossip, too. "That you claimed he stole your ideas and patented them himself. It seems to me, in light of all this," she waved at the physically pretty but rather unassuming seeming possible murder weapon, "is excellent motive for murder."

How ironic the TV show itself was about deadly plants. Or maybe that was the point. While I struggled to accept Sandra would kill Halliwell, it did make sense, didn't it?

"I admit it," Sandra said suddenly, voice trembling, tears now spilling down her cheeks, "we were in love once. No," she chopped one hand through the air, "*I* was in love. He used me. He betrayed me. But I'm not a murderer. I would never use one of our precious plants to kill someone like him." It sounded to me like doing so would be the biggest insult to the plant ever. Which said a lot about how she felt about him.

"I'm sorry, Sandra," Cherise said, "but I'm going to have to ask you to come down to the station and answer some more questions. If you agree to come with me, I won't have to use these." She tugged out her cuffs, let them dangle, while Sandra stared at them in growing horror and understanding.

"You don't say a word," Thalia spun on her, "until my lawyers," yup, plural, because money, yo, "get there. I mean it, Sandra. Not one more word." She faced down the sheriff with the most courage and self-possession I'd ever seen from Thalia before. "I trust you won't badger her until she has proper representation, Sheriff King?"

Now, Cherise was my best friend and Thalia had known her for years. Adored her daughter, Layla, had dinner at my house and around Wallace. She wasn't a stranger, a far cry from it. But the way Thalia confronted the sheriff had my heart sighing in sorrow that things had come to this.

Cherise could have pushed back. She was well within her rights to do so, being sheriff and all, and Thalia's family's reputation for shoving said sheriff around one of those horrible historical events I still hadn't heard the whole truth of. Cherise had to have felt the sting of a Vesterville—even the lovely one I knew and adored—trying to interfere with her job.

I shouldn't have worried, however. I knew better. Because, like the truly amazing and compassionate woman I knew her to be, her Amazonian proportions and her penchant for intimidating all of those who deserved it notwithstanding, Cherise King had the kindest heart of anyone I knew. And showed it, in that moment, leaning into the steadfast girl she'd also watched grow into the woman she was. Gave her the space to feel it.

"Thalia," Cherise said, barely chiding. Stopped. Waited patiently and graciously. While Thalia flushed, slowly, embarrassment crossing her face, shame, before she threw her arms around the sheriff.

"I'm sorry," she said. Pulled back when Cherise let her go. "It's just… Cherise, Sandra's my friend. She wouldn't kill anyone, I'm positive of it."

"I know she's your friend," Cherise said. "I trust your judgment." Thalia bowed her head to that. It had to help since Thalia was a Vesterville and the sheriff's history with that family had troubles I'm positive the young heiress knew about. "That's why I'm asking, Lia, and not jumping to conclusions. I *have* to ask, it's my job." She relented, pulled away, giving Thalia space from the pressure of her presence, courteous and gentle or not. Cherise was still imposing even when she loved you. "I'm on your side, I promise." Her tone didn't change, though the words held their own threat. "But Sandra, if you killed Halliwell Thicket, if you had anything at all to do with his death, I promise you, I'll find out." The gardener stiffened, Thalia reaching for her with a shaking hand. "And I also promise you, it'll go easier on you if you tell the truth now."

Sandra shook her head, lips pressed tightly together, taking Thalia's original advice to heart. And preceded the sheriff when Cherise gestured for her to exit the poison garden for the main event space and her car in the lot.

Thalia and I followed all the way to Cherise's black Charger, Thalia waiting for the sheriff to help Sandra into the back before turning and hugging me.

"We might as well cancel the event now,"

she said. "This disaster has to end."

"If you don't mind," Cherise said, "I'd prefer you carry on." That had both of us staring at the sheriff who shrugged. "If you're right, Lia, and Sandra isn't guilty, I'd rather the real killer didn't get away. Give me a bit, at least until tomorrow."

I waved her off as she drove away, turning to Thalia whose blue eyes brimmed with tears. She reached out and slid the sunglasses down my nose, looked in my eyes. I put all my love and compassion and support in my gaze, letting her soak it in before she pushed the mirrored aviators back into place and sighed.

"We'll do as the sheriff asks," she said. "But my heart's not in it, Seph. I'm going to go call my lawyers now. Can you tell Callie where I went?"

"I'll take care of everything," I said. "Why don't you go keep Bella company for a bit? I think she's lonely and could use the company." Never mind the maids were probably mauling her as usual. Seemed like a good suggestion, though, and had the young woman nodding in agreement.

Thalia left, walking with ponderous slowness up the path toward the estate house, and I was so focused on her I missed his approach until he stood beside me, observing her.

"Anything I should worry about?" Jason pivoted toward me, though he didn't make a move, just waited to see what I'd do. Did he expect me to just tell him everything and swoon and bat my eyelashes when life and death was on the table?

He might think his charm had me in knots—and maybe it did at times—but if he thought I was that shallow and careless he had sorely misread me. This was one time that hormones and gossip weren't going to win because Thalia was far, far more important.

"Headache," I lied on purpose and didn't give a crap if he knew it. Shrugged. "You know. Rich girls these days." Let him meet my flat and uncompromising gaze over the top of his own glasses still perched on my face, feel the weight of the silence, take in my resistance to his ability to convince me to tell him anything at all that would compromise the people I loved. Because he wasn't on that list and just lost his chance to find out if he'd ever make it there.

He squinted at me then, mouth twisting, any attempt to connive or charm me gone as he silently accepted my rebellion and decided to switch tactics. "It was murder," he said, no question, all confidence. "And the sheriff thinks Sandra Lin did it." Again with the solid certainty, which meant he was either smart enough to put it together or someone talked.

Didn't matter which, not really. I figured he had the brainpower to assemble the pieces knowing what he did about Halliwell and the life he chose to lead. If one of Cherise's deputies spoke out of turn, that was her problem. Right now, mine was making sure Thalia was protected. So, I didn't respond, wanting to make sure she got away before he could chase her down, knowing he wouldn't try if I was standing there. "The whole reason I'm here is the Halliwell-Sandra scandal." Ah, so he finally decided to change tactics and be honest? I glanced at him out of the corner of his sunglasses, Thalia disappearing behind a shrub.

"Good for you," I said, knowing the shade I threw likely put me on his crap list and not caring. Come at me, bro. I was done with being treated like a target. "Maybe you should talk to the sheriff, then. I'm sure she'd be happy for any evidence you can provide." I handed back his aviators and walked away, no longer interested in banter or flirting.

I had to find my daughter.

CHAPTER ELEVEN

As I strode through the crowd, no one commented on Sandra's departure, the talk of the times all about Tansy's missing plant. While at first, I thought perhaps Tansy's outburst was just the top of the list, I quickly realized the gardener's disappearance hadn't been noticed as of yet. Big sigh of relief, let me tell you. At least we dodged that bullet, for the time being, a bare scrape through of a win, but I'd take it.

Though when I almost collided with Calliope, it was clear she at least had heard the news, her reaction strong enough I worried my daughter might pull a Tansy on me and have the whole crowd in the know in short order.

"*Mom*," she said. "This is *horrible*." I almost shut her down, but she did it herself, shuddering and hugging her arms around her torso, hazel eyes full of tears. Her voice lowered, however, steadied and I knew she had to be thinking about her girlfriend and the implications of Sandra's departure with Cherise. "Where's Lia?" Yup, there it was, the inevitable question and, honestly, the one I wanted her to ask because putting Thalia first meant Calliope would hold it together to make sure the dear Vesterville heiress didn't suffer further.

Sometimes putting others first was all we had.

"She went back to the house to lie down," I said, keeping my voice low. "Cherise wants the event to carry on just in case the real killer is still here." I shuddered at that idea, my kid doing the same. "Thalia needs to step away and I don't blame her. Can we do this without her and Sandra?" That was the question, right? Could we? I almost considered calling the rest of the event off, of stepping back and chucking the rest of this complicated and disastrous attempt at my daughter and her girlfriend doing something together.

Which meant, of course, we'd be doing no such thing.

Calliope's face firmed while my resolve did. "Sure, we can," she said. "I already have Sandra's plan. And Thalia really just wanders around and talks to people." Her eyes widened further, head shaking. "She's totally necessary."

I laughed at that. "Honey, I get it. It's a good thing. As long as we know what to do next, it should go smoothly." I wished I felt as confident as I sounded.

Calliope, for her part, buoyed which actually helped me more than she would know, gaze alight, chin lifting. "We got this, Mom," she said. Hesitated, sadness crossing her face. "Mom…"

"May I offer assistance?" I turned in surprise to see Pearl had closed in on us, though I had no idea how much she'd overheard. While battling the irritation she'd intruded just when Calliope seemed on the brink of saying something I hoped fell along the lines of *I love you, I forgive you, I'm sorry.* Instead, I got to listen to Pearl carry on. "I noticed another of our judges is… indisposed so I'm jumping to an obvious conclusion." She waved off our mutual silence after a moment with a clear laugh that surprised me, her pale eyes sparkling. "I know I lay it on a little thick," she said, voice low now, leaning in, "but I'm not as horrible as all that. It's part of the show. People expect it."

The old fox, I knew it. "I'd appreciate it if you'd keep your guesses to yourself."

She nodded quickly. "Of course, my dear. While I have no love for Halliwell and really can't bring myself to mourn his passing, Sandra Lin is a talented and brilliant woman who never should have fallen prey to that… man." She sniffed. "So, if I can help in any way to assist you while the sheriff finds her innocent, I'm happy to do so."

Calliope grinned, far more open and understanding than I'd ever been at her age, hopefully a sign I'd done a good job (while knowing I had). "Welcome to the team."

I glanced up as she and Pearl shook hands, noting Jason Arnold talking with Tansy Powers, his phone aimed at her, likely recording her as he interviewed her about the theft. While I could have let things go, I took a few steps closer, doing my best to be circumspect and knowing I was about as obvious as I could get because my sneaking skills frankly sucked. Only then did I notice Darren standing on the outside of his booth, face a bit pale, talking quickly into his own phone as he turned sideways when a knot of guests walked too close.

Hmmm. What was he up to? I forgot all about Jason and Tansy, choosing instead to snoop on someone who wouldn't see me approach not out of any ability I had but because he had his back turned. Giving me the moment I needed to slide in behind him and eavesdrop.

I didn't know for sure he was up to no good, but the way this weekend was going? It certainly crossed my mind he might be involved in one or both crimes.

"You don't understand," he was saying in a hurried whisper. "I can't now. The thing went missing. It's too dangerous to hand it over with the original gone."

While the details were clearly missing, the gist came through rather clearly and had my suspicions raised. I naturally drew all kinds of assumptions while knowing he could have been talking about something at work and I completely misconstrued the whole one-sided conversation. But before he went on and clarified further so I could jump on him with an authoritative *ah-ha!* (or, more likely, slide away in guilty regret I'd misjudged him), Darren glanced over his shoulder, saw me nearby and flinched.

Oh, that flinch spoke volumes of guilty information that had me firmly in the *told you so* camp. What it was, however, that might be worthy of such snide satisfaction I had, as yet, to discover. And wouldn't be now, thanks to his suspicion and my lacking in the spying department. I waved a little in a vain effort to pretend I hadn't been snooping, knowing I wasn't fooling a soul when the rep swiftly ending the call then hurried past me and back into the relative safety of his booth.

That was fine with me. I wasn't qualified, really, to go digging anyway and had proven that not so long ago with a suspected drug dealer who'd put a wedge between me and my sheriff friend. Okay, I was guilty of the distance created, because I'd tried to talk to someone I wasn't supposed to talk to without help and pretty much made Cherise's life uncomfortable without reason. So, I was more than happy to leave the interrogation to her. Cherise could ask him some pointed questions with the information I had as leverage, as little as it was. I was happy enough making him wriggle and squirm thinking I overheard more than I did, just to soften him up for her.

Delicious really, how fun this investigating thing could be when it really shouldn't have been.

I rejoined Pearl and Calliope who had obviously been in the midst of hammering out some kind of responsibility deal while I frowned at Darren then turned back. "Sandra mentioned that rare plant theft happens at events like this."

Pearl nodded, tsking in Tansy's direction. "Poor dear. It's terrible and happens far too frequently. Not just at events, but from private greenhouses, even. The thing is, though, the thieves never take the full plant, so this is odd."

"What do they take?" Calliope sounded as curious and confused as I felt.

"Slips," Pearl said. "Big enough to grow another version of the plant." She must have read the continuing loss in our comprehension because she went on. "Rare hybrids, especially one-of-a-kinds, can go for tens of thousands of dollars to collectors. Hundreds of thousands, even. Everything from leaves worth $15,000 for a single sample for medical research to legacy flowers with pure lineages, stealing slips is the most lucrative because it doesn't do damage to the plant, only the plant's owners and creators, eliminating the rarity and lowering the value while lining the pockets of the thieves and giving the collectors what they want."

I had kept Darren in my periphery the whole time she talked and noted it when he left his booth and hurried off. Pearl glared after him, impossible to miss, as she spoke again.

"The poor girl. I didn't get much of a look, but the plant seemed unique. She could have had a real winner."

"I thought her grandmother was a fraud and a hack," I said without pulling the sarcasm even a little bit.

Pearl's nose scrunched when she grinned, rather adorable now that I knew for sure she wasn't the horrible person she pretended to be for the masses. "The show, my dear. Remember the show. What else is there?" Aged or not, when the older woman spread her arms to encompass the experience, she lost ten years off her face, smile delightful. I shouldn't have been enjoying the fact she purposely made people uncomfortable, I suppose, but she took such joy in the moment I smiled in return. "Besides, if Lydia was judging me or mine, she'd say the same thing." Okay, that did make me feel better. She released her humor for more regret. "The saddest part isn't financial, despite what you might think. Though the loss could mean a huge hit for her and her name, for Lydia's greenhouse. It's costly to support such creation and the payback can often mean the difference between developing new strains and being forced into more commercial aspects of the business to stay afloat." Her blue eyes reflected the sunlight, almost translucent. "And yet, even worse? If it *was* a new hybrid, it could have set Tansy up with the prestige she needed for sponsorship, which would mean she could abandon that side of the business altogether. Focus on her research and development." It sounded like Pearl might have had that very opportunity herself at one time. "These days, sponsors mean funding and support, not to mention travel to attend larger, international events, which only increases the chance of continuing success." She looked back to me, lips thinned in regret. "Such a loss may even be once in a lifetime. To make her mark. A terrible tragedy for someone meant to do this work." Again, she sounded like she took it very personally. Had she lost such a chance herself once upon a time?

"Pearl," I said, "do you know anyone who would have wanted to hurt Halliwell Thicket?" Yes, I know, it sounded like everyone hated him, but I was looking for specifics. And I was thinking theft, now, trying to tie pieces together that didn't quite fit, knowing it sounded like I was changing the subject when I really wasn't.

Could Halliwell be involved in the thefts, maybe working to identify ideal candidates and shared information with those who did the deed? Or be the slip thief himself and thus created a motive for his own murder? Could Tansy have killed him? I did see her near the greenhouse, but that didn't mean she'd poisoned him. Then again, she wasn't the only one who had a plant stolen, just the only one *here*. Could one or more of the other growers be holding a grudge as yet uncovered?

Pearl didn't seem to mind the question, instead pausing to think about it, then glancing over her shoulder again to where Darren had hurried off. "There was a rumor," she said, her mind still on the topic she'd been talking about, "that Darren Moorehead has had something to do with the slip thefts, but there's no proof. I do know he befriends growers and has been pretty close with several who lost slips." She shrugged just a little. "You're wondering why I switched the topic back, but I didn't. Because the rumor? Came from Halliwell, just last night."

CHAPTER TWELVE

Well now, wasn't that interesting. "Can you tell me what monkshood tastes like?" Her thin and pale eyebrows shot up so fast I knew I was giving away a lot more than I meant to. "Humor me."

She shifted her feet, tucking her cardigan around her thin frame, face suddenly pinched and wrinkled gaze narrowed. "Bitter," she said. "Horrendously bitter. So much so no one in their right mind would drink enough of it to cause their death."

"Unless," I countered, "that someone had a hankering for bitter drinks and even used them to taunt people. Wouldn't that sort of negate the taste issue?"

Pearl's nod was barely perceptible. "You think someone gave him monkshood." I didn't respond and she gusted out a sigh, looking away. "Yes, very possible. The man was a fool and a noisy, cranky, nasty person who didn't understand the game at all. He meant his hurtfulness, whereas I only play a part. I despised him, we all did. But killing him with one of our precious plants…" She shrugged then, chin up, shoulders squared. "Perhaps it's poetic justice, at that." She glanced back and forth between myself and the quietly watchful Calliope. "I noticed you have monkshood here in the estate garden. It seems to me if someone did have an inclination it could have been a simple act of sabotage."

"You drank from the glass," I said, not wanting to worry her. While still worrying about her even though I already knew better because I'd been down this road of concern for myself and others (including her). Forget that she stood, healthy and breathing, in front of me and he was dead.

She brushed that off because *logic*, Persephone. "If I had a lethal dose, my dear, or a dose of any measure, I'd be long ill or dead by now." See? Nothing at all to worry about. However, her frown led me to believe she was more anxious about it than she was willing to admit. Well, fair enough, considering had she chosen—had we all chosen—to partake of the disgusting drink later in the night things could have turned out very differently with a lot of ill people and maybe two corpses instead of just Halliwell in the morgue.

Was it wrong to call that a win? It was, right? Yeah, thought so.

"We have an event to run," Calliope said then, her need to leap into action visible in her body, in the command of her tone that I'd never heard from her before. This new and grown-up version of my daughter would take getting used to, but I wasn't complaining. "This really is kind of Cherise's job, Mom, while ours isn't getting done when it needs our attention." Wow, okay, kiddo, hold your freaking horses there a second.

And yet, true enough. I just would rather not endure chastisement from my twenty-one-year-old (almost twenty-two, but who's counting) when we were still kind of on a bit of a brink. Instead of arguing with her or lingering on things I couldn't change (yes, I let it go, imagine), I nodded, stepped back and carried on to the end of the day.

While Calliope led Pearl away, chattering with the old woman and leaving me behind.

Not hurt. Not bitter. *Not.*

Uh-huh.

Since the merchant booths closed at 5PM

and the barbeque fired up an hour later, I didn't have much longer to walk my beat anyway, and the time went surprisingly quickly for all. Probably because I was so busy overthinking what happened while trying to do Cherise's job regardless of what Calliope said or I thought.

You try shutting off your brain when murder and theft and your kid's safety are involved. See how far it gets you. I'll wait.

To my surprise, the transition from the presentations to the wrap-up of the market to the family fun event happened easily and effortlessly. A credit to Sandra's plan, maybe, but I gave most of it to my kid who seemed to be everywhere at once with her lovely smile and firm control and endless energy I wished I could muster.

By the time the evening's barbeque was fully underway, I was ready for a nap, the final event of the day a roaring success, in my estimation. Small children ran amok over the estate front lawn, the parking lot packed, the smoking grills delivering all kinds of goodies until well after 8PM. I looked up from helping one of the caterers flip a giant rack of ribs to see Sandra striding toward me, clearly released from custody.

I joined her when she motioned for me to do so, pulling me aside, tucking us behind a towering oak tree, Sandra shaking and visibly angry.

"She let you go," I said. "That has to be a good sign."

"She only did so because Thalia's lawyers bullied her into it." Sandra's hands fisted at her sides, her body swaying as though she resisted the urge to pace or punch something (hopefully not me or the tree, poor tree). "I didn't kill Halliwell, Seph, I swear it. But all the evidence looks so bad." Now tears welled again, and her anger shifted into fear, a typical response to threat.

"I believe you, Sandra," I said, still not sure I did but knowing she'd be more pliable and willing to talk if I convinced her. That had her nodding, relaxing just enough I could carry on with reasonable expectation. Yes, I was deceiving her a little. Yes, I felt bad about it. Yes, I'd pay for it sometime, probably. But right now, if I could get her to tell me what happened, maybe she was innocent, and her truth could not only set her free but catch the real killer.

Keep telling yourself stuff like that, Pringle. Whatever helps you sleep at night.

"All of it is true," she said. "Halliwell stole my ideas, it's not really a big secret. I just dropped it because I didn't want to have to deal with him or any of it anymore. It broke me, Seph, his betrayal." She collapsed to the ground, back pressed to the tree, while I sat next to her and held space. "That's why I left the circuit, not out of shame or embarrassment like everyone thinks. I lost my love for the work for a while. A long while." She blinked, a trembling smile pulling at her lips. "And then I met Thalia and she offered me this job. I had to take it. Realized I had never really lost my passion for it. I just needed distance."

My phone buzzed and, knowing who it probably was, I checked it when Sandra nodded it was okay.

"Cherise," I said, deciding to be open about it rather than hiding who I spoke to. Sandra had to know it was her anyway. "She needs a sample of the plant from the estate to compare to the poison in the bottle. The lab says they can positively ID the exact one the toxin came from."

Sandra stood, brushing at the seat of her pants with a resigned expression. "I'll gather that for her," she said, waving off my unspoken protest. "Don't worry, I'll take Pearl with me. Will that satisfy your need for transparency, or should I allow the deputies to mangle what Thalia and I have worked so hard to build?" She swallowed, looked away. "I'm sorry, Seph.

This isn't your fault. It seems like every time I try to create something, it falls apart and there's nothing I can do to fix it."

She had to be talking about Halliwell, her history with him, the loss of the show and her designs. How hard had it been for her to pick herself up and start again? To trust Thalia and take the plunge when she'd faced failure and betrayal from the man she loved? Couldn't have been easy for a woman I had no doubt held herself to the highest standard and, I knew, adored Thalia as much as I did. Letting herself down wouldn't hold a candle to ruining things for her employer.

Before I could say anything of comfort, however, she met my eyes, her expression begging me to keep it to myself, to let her do what she needed to do. I took in her silent plea for trust and understanding and nodded. Let her go, knowing Cherise wouldn't have agreed but not willing to undercut the trust I'd built because honestly? I really didn't like Sandra for the murder. Yes, she was still hurting, but that kind of calculated and horrible end, it felt fresh. Her pain was old and as she'd said, she found peace and love of plants again. Why would she risk that?

Unless he'd said something to her that triggered her.

All thoughts about poisons and murderers and everything else fled my mind at the sight of the bounding white cat leaping her way over the hedge at the corner of the estate house and heading—you guessed it—back toward the last place in the world she should have been going.

What was she thinking? Nothing, she was a freaking cat and she wanted me to die of heart failure at her expense because she didn't care about anyone but herself.

Irrationality in the face of more frustration? Check.

I gave chase with a grunt and a soft swearword I won't repeat in this company, already tired but spurred on by fresh adrenaline—I was going to run out at any point, and it would be Belladonna's fault—and the knowledge that the contrary feline would get herself killed just to spite me.

Lucky for me, the escaped prisoner decided a detour behind the greenhouse was much more to her liking than putting her life at risk in the poisoned garden (so she had some sense, at least), which meant she avoided certain near-death this time. I stress, this time. At least, I hoped so because who knew what kind of mischief she was about to get herself into that could risk life and limb?

When I skidded around the hedge in hot

pursuit of my frustrating feline, I found myself sliding to a halt in shock at the sight of her sitting like a queen waiting for her court to fawn on her and bring her crown.

Trying to be stately (and succeeding, where many would fail) while perched on the steaming compost pile.

I admit, the comic relief? Epic. I laughed out loud.

"You're getting filthy," I said, still snort-giggling at the sight of her trying to carry on her arrogant dominance from the middle of a heap of decaying plant matter and discarded sod. "If you don't come down here right now, you'll have to have a bath." She blinked at that. "And you know you hate baths."

Contrary and conniving creature. She flicked her tail at me, climbed higher when I drew close. Naturally. Because nothing would please Her Majesty more than to see me have to slip and slide my way through the same filth she bounded over with delicate precision. Just to prove her commitment, she sat again, barely out of reach. Forcing me to climb the scraps of sod and grass clippings and hopefully nothing too disgusting (they wouldn't use this for household stuff, right? Ew), having to paw my way a few handholds to pull myself up.

She finally let me catch her, hugging her

tight as the two of us slid down the side of the pile, my clothes filthy, my cat covered in dirt and debris. As I turned to try to brush some of it free, my gaze fell on something that had been worked loose from the compost when I'd disturbed the surface.

And, with my heart soaring suddenly and a mystery solved—though an odd ending to it— I hefted Belladonna in one arm and the remains of Tansy's plant in the other before plodding my triumphant and filthy way back to the event grounds.

Turns out I wasn't the only master detective in our family. Though I was pretty sure the cat who wriggled her protest every step of the way would have purrfurred (yeah, I went there) to remain anonymous.

CHAPTER THIRTEEN

The apologetic maid didn't get nearly enough of my attention when she appeared in a flustered huff, arms outstretched for the cat I handed off with a forehead kiss of thanks. Because I wasn't mad, couldn't be, crossing to the greenhouse, spotting Thalia (wasn't she supposed to be resting? No one listened to me) talking with the woman of the hour. Honestly, I was surprised she was getting a word in edgewise considering the state Tansy had been in the last time I saw her. From the redness of her cheeks and the impatient expression on her face, she wasn't going to be silent much longer.

That was until she saw what I had for her. I just hoped the poor plant wasn't on its last legs or this victory march could turn into another fresh disaster.

"—so sorry and if there's anything I can do to compensate you, Tansy." Thalia's hands shook, visibly distraught, which only amped up my excitement as I stomped triumphantly into their presence, offering up the plant—an offering I'd now convinced myself for Thalia's sake was only a little worse for wear but still alive and kicking, surely—to the startled young woman who it belonged to.

"I found your plant!" I was so pleased with myself I almost missed the panic on her face, the way she paled so much she swayed, Thalia reaching out to catch her while Tansy refused—outright refused—to touch the thing I tried to hand off.

Hang on a second. I'd climbed a compost heap for this thing. The least she could do was be grateful. And yes, I'd also climbed said heap for my cat, but that was beside the point.

"No, you can't—" She looked back and forth between us so quickly she stumbled, swayed again. "What have you done? This can't be happening."

Um. Done? Saved your stupid creation, child. You're freaking welcome. But I had a feeling, as Thalia guided Tansy through the entrance to the greenhouse and sat her on the edge of one of the displays before she fell down, that there was much more to discover around the disappearance and supposed (yeah, I said it) theft of the hybrid in question than Tansy was willing to admit.

The fact Thalia tucked her out of the way of prying eyes? Meant she had to be thinking what I was thinking. That Tansy hadn't exactly been honest with us and her freak out might have another purpose and this discovery wasn't in her plan.

I was done being lied to, deceived and conned. She'd be ponying up the truth or I'd be calling Cherise lickety-split because no one who made such a big deal the way she had of losing supposed valuable property should look at the plant I held in my hands like she looked at it. Time she faced the thing she'd just been making a huge deal out of.

"Spill it," I said, my patience gone, Thalia's startled reaction to my anger not a chastisement but true surprise. Sure, I rarely lost my temper this way, but I was at my limit, tired and hot and dirty and sick of plants and corpses and cats who couldn't stay freaking put for five minutes.

And, frankly, over all of this so much I could just *scream*.

Temper, temper, Persephone Pringle.

I kind of expected Tansy to shout at me, to fall back into the angry and tirade-driven tear-soaked song and dance she'd been practicing since she accused someone of taking her precious and yet now abhorrent creation. Instead of pushback, however, she shocked me by bursting into tears. But not the furious kind she'd used as a weapon earlier. Nope, this ugly manifestation of truth had her rocking and broken. And while I'd liked her when we first met and had the instinct to protect her from Pearl and Halliwell's cruelty? She'd lost a lot of my sympathy when she came for Thalia. Which meant even this genuine outpouring of grief and what felt like regret didn't soften all my angst. I do admit to some rays of compassion working their way through like beams through a cloud. Because those tears were real ones, I was sure, genuine sobs and guilt and hurt that was impossible to ignore crossing her face.

"It's a fraud," she said, gulping around her weeping. "The plant, it's a fake." Thalia stared down at it in her own horror as I dropped it at Tansy's feet. "I made it up. There's no such thing as a rainbow hibiscus." I was staring right at it, and still didn't understand. "I created it to catch the thief, not to win or fool anyone, not forever. But nothing went the way it was supposed to and now this…" she gestured at the discarded remains of her failed plot. "Now everything is all just a disaster."

Thalia sat next to her, gentle, holding her hands, kind to her while I fought off my indecision about whether I was going to relent or not.

Of course, I relented. Eventually.

"Tell us what happened, Tansy." No, my tone wasn't exactly kind. Which had Thalia looking up at me, the woman she'd become behind those eyes, a far cry from the girl I knew, helped raise. Realized I'd kind of been a good influence on her, too, and relaxed my antagonism, nodded. Let her take the lead while I stepped off, breathing long and deep while Thalia handled her fellow grower.

"My grandmother," Tansy said. "She's been creating hybrids for years. But every time she had a success, every time she went to a show, someone stole a slip or took the whole plant. She even had someone raid her greenhouse at home." More tears trickled, but this time Tansy wiped angrily at them. "Every single creation devalued thanks to the thief or thieves who used her talent to make them rich. But she never complained, not once, and she refused to stop creating. She said nature gave her the gift to tie blossoms together into new life and fame and money didn't have to be part of it."

Okay, I liked her grandmother a lot. Had a feeling Lydia Powers and I would get along swimmingly. "So, she wouldn't approve of what you had planned, I take it."

"Gran has no idea what I'm doing," Tansy said. "She can't ever know." Grief caught hold, silenced her a moment, stripping away her ability to breathe, to speak. When she was able to draw a jagged breath, she caught it and went on through cracking and warbling words. "No one ever cared. There were rumors, but no one did anything. The police don't think it's a real case and the organizers stuff it under the sod because they don't want anyone to know what's really going on."

Thalia nodded slowly. "That made you try to catch the culprit yourself."

Tansy stared down at her hands, drawing another deep breath, this one shaking but filling her lungs at least. "I created a target." She shrugged, wiping her nose with the hem of her golf shirt. "I brought the fake with me, made a big deal about it beforehand, as much as I could. Then waited for the thief to try to take a slip."

"But Halliwell's death interfered?" I thought about her sneaking behind the greenhouse and had a horrible thought. "Tansy, was Halliwell the thief? Did you poison him?"

Her head jerked up, huge, hazel eyes almost

bulging. "What? No! I would never." She licked her lips. "It didn't happen like that. I was too late." That came out in a wailing protest. "Before he even died, or I knew about it. I came to the greenhouse to wait for the thief, but it was too late. The slip was already gone." She sagged in defeat. "I don't know how I missed it, but I did. So, the only thing I had left was to make a stink. I dumped the plant and pretended it was stolen so maybe the thief would be uncovered if the organizers took the loss seriously." She reached out and squeezed Thalia's hand. "I'm sorry. It's not your fault. I was just so frustrated. I shouldn't have treated you that way."

Thalia's firm headshake was followed by conviction. "I'm the one who failed you, Tansy," she said. "Your property should have been safe here and it wasn't. That's on me and this event." She sighed then, rubbing at her face with her free hand, that headache I'd told Jason she suffered from probably a reality now. "So, you buried it in the compost to hide it."

Tansy released her fingers, sat up straighter. "I wanted to destroy it completely, but there were so many people around and when I finally got it out of the greenhouse, I was almost caught so many times I figured if I buried it and went back for it I could do the job then." She stared up at me. "I never thought in a million years anyone would find it."

"She's a pain in the butt like that," I said, waving off Tansy's confusion, making a wry face at Thalia. "Bella got out. This was her doing."

The young heiress managed a small smile. "We need to do something about this, Seph. We can't let the thief get away."

"With the plant returned to me, it's over," Tansy said.

"Maybe," I said slowly, thinking it over. "Maybe not." I looked down at the fake at my feet. "What makes it a fraud?"

Tansy lifted the plant, showed Thalia and me where she'd carefully glued blossoms onto stems they didn't belong to, the hibiscus petals artistically painted with inks that didn't damage the velvet of the petals but was clearly fake on closer inspection. "It wouldn't have passed judging," she said, "but I never thought I'd get to Pearl and Halliwell anyway. I figured the thief would be caught and I could rub it in their face that they tried to steal a fake." She set it in her lap, the poor lopsided thing falling to pieces like the plan she'd created. "I'm so tired of my grandmother's hard work being stolen. Even if it's not about prestige or money, it's still wrong."

While I didn't have any proof? I was fairly confident I knew how to fix this, or, at the very least, put an end to it continuing in the future. Took the plant from Tansy and gave it a once-over squint before fixing her with a determined stare.

"Mind if I take this?" She shook her head in surprise, Thalia rising to her feet.

"You have an idea." That amused and happy gleam was back in my second daughter's eyes, hope rising in the young woman beside her when she, too, stood.

"What are you going to do?" Tansy's tears had dried up, hands clenched before her. I debated filling them both in but decided against it. Not because I didn't trust them (okay, Tansy) not to run off and ruin the surprise I had planned, but because there was someone else who needed to know the details first and I didn't have a whole lot of time and it would all burn up if I had to go through it twice.

"I think I might have a plan," I said. Grinned suddenly, though this wasn't fun, and I wasn't looking forward to payback. Never mind I'd agreed to not make myself a pain in Cherise's butt by asking questions of those I really needed to steer clear of. She'd be thanking me when this was over, I was sure of it. "You two pretend nothing happened. I'm going to go see someone about a missing plant." Nope, no fun unfolding here, move along, nothing to see. Just a holistic therapist and a fake hibiscus out for a stroll.

Yeah, I know. I was enjoying this a little too much. Figured I had it coming, though, so while I dialed back on the grin of satisfaction, I let the expectation of success refuel me.

Why was it one mystery often folded into another until I felt like they'd never end? Well, at least this one I could solve, but only if the hurried encounter right here at the greenhouse last night tied to the rumor I'd been told and the phone call I'd overheard meant what I thought it did. Was pretty sure they all led to one person and one person only.

Sure, I was no Cherise King. But even I could put two and two together and come up with Darren Moorehead.

CHAPTER FOURTEEN

He was behind the counter, on the phone again, his two employees gone for the evening, the merchant area closed up and abandoned by the crowds from earlier in the day. I figured I'd find him there, happy to have him cornered and with enough privacy to carry out my plan. Sure, a little thrill of fear and excitement went hand in hand with that emotion, but what I hoped was about to unfold would be worth it if things turned out the way I intended.

Yes, best-laid plans. On my mind, trust me. Didn't stop me, though. When I entered the booth, Darren Moorehead looked up, visibly surprised, not attempting a reflexive smile, his gaze dropping to the plant in my hands.

The instant his face fell in terror, I dropped the fraudulent creation on the ground between us with a smile before taking his phone from his unresisting hand.

"He'll have to call you back. He's about to be arrested." I hung up on whoever was on the other end of the line, almost grinning because how fun was that to say out loud? Darren fish lipped, my favorite, while I pushed the plant toward him with one foot, the rep backing away from it until he was pressed to the pile of boxes at the rear of the tent. "Isn't that right, Darren? For theft? A lot of thefts." I nudged Tansy's fake hybrid one last time until it covered his right shoe, lying there in limp accusation. "Except, this time the slip you took? From this particular plant?" His gaze dropped to that now rather hideous collection of leaves and stems and crushed blossoms all clinging valiantly to the root system emerging from what was left of the soil that had been meant to give it life. "Not like anything else you've ever tried to sell to the highest bidder. And is about to get you the justice you deserve." A lot to ask of a plant, but I knew it was up to the task.

The only question that remained—was I? We were about to find out.

Darren tried to deny it, gaze snapping to the side of the tent, but I was in the way. For how much longer, I wasn't sure. He was bigger than me, and if he chose to muscle past me and exit, I'd be out of luck. To my surprise, however, he stayed, maybe out of guilt, or perhaps that intimidation Jason Arnold mentioned wasn't a joke. I know I felt about as powerful as an avenging goddess standing there, calling him to task for his wrongdoing, while he crumbled like a clay statue under the pressure.

"I should let you sell that slip," I said, pointing at Tansy's plant. "It'll ruin you. But I'd rather have the police handle that."

"Ruin me?" He managed to squeak that out.

"That's right, you don't know everything." I nudged it again, Darren flinching from it as though it might leap up and bite him. "Like the fact Tansy created it, not by growing it, but patchworking pieces together to build something a thief couldn't resist." His gaze flickered again to the thing at his feet, back to me, understanding dawning in his dark eyes. "A trap, long thought out and conceived out of frustration." I tilted my head, faked curiosity. "Can you imagine just how frustrated she'd become, Darren? Can you comprehend just how desperate your decision to steal from her made her? What it drove her to?" I shrugged in carefully contrived casualness. "I can. And I'm sure the police will agree when they sit you down to explain why it is you thought you could get away with ruining others for the sake of your own gain."

He shifted his weight, sullen anger rising at last. "You can't prove anything."

"Oh, but I *can*," I said. "Thanks to Tansy. Who came here with the express purpose of catching the thief who's been stripping her grandmother's creations for years. Not to mention the hard work of all the others you took from. You do know it could only go on so long? That someone was bound to catch on?"

His lower lip quivered, body sagging a little, the coward in him showing up and, frankly, making him more dangerous. "It's *fake*?" The fact he fixated on that detail had me hoping he did sell the slip and was now in deeper trouble with his clients than he could even be with the police.

"She fabricated the whole thing," I said with a smile. "Just to catch you. But she wanted *you*, not to ruin you with your clients. Her goal was for you to get caught, Darren. Punished." I let that sink in. "So, when you beat her to the take, when she realized she'd failed to catch you in the act, she tried to draw attention to the theft the only way she knew how." I toed the plant one more time. "Except, from what I hear, she could have just waited it out. Because the rumor is that Halliwell Thicket had your ticket, Darren." I was taking a huge chance here, and though I wasn't sure he was the killer, it made sense to throw it into the mix, right? Stir things just a little more and see if guilt surfaced. Sure, it did. A *wonderful* idea. Oh, boy. "Was that why you murdered him?" Oh, those words got a reaction, you better believe it, a herky-jerky flinching response on the border between denial and culpability. *Was* he the killer? That would just be the peach. "I know when you stole the slip." He started, my purposeful bounding from one idea to the next a tailored experience just for him, meant to keep him off-balance, in an effort to shimmy loose whatever it was he'd done.

Looked like I was right on target, the way he shook his head, lips slack, but I carried on as if he hadn't reacted because more pressure was needed, and I was far from done.

"I ran into you just after you took it. Didn't I?" That was met with nothing, and it didn't matter, anyway. I already knew it was true. His reaction to me last night, the way he'd seemed rushed and nervous when I'd run into him outside the greenhouse, all pointed to perfect timing and a stolen slip—not to mention slip-up. "You'd already done the deed to Halliwell's bottle, long before the theft. Right?" Okay, now his lack of response had me second-guessing my tactic. He stared at me, eyes bulging, and I feared perhaps I'd pushed him too hard. Nothing to be done for it, though. I carried on and hoped he'd crack before he, well. *Cracked*, if you know what I mean. "You poisoned him earlier in the evening. Found out about the deadly garden and knew it was the perfect choice. The ironic choice." I carefully monitored the florid peak of red in his cheeks, the rest of his face so pale and sweaty I feared for his heart, the way it pulsed under his skin at his neck in rapid-fire beating far too quickly for sustained good health. "Of course, you know all about monkshood. You've been in the business a long time. Had to be aware the bitter taste would be masked by his favorite drink. You wandered into the unlocked garden, dug up a slip of the plant and dosed his bottle." I pointed across the way, ever so close, to Halliwell's booth. Location was everything. "You saw where he kept his stash, so you snuck into his booth and dosed the bottle and killed the one person who knew for certain you were the thief. And then carried on as if you hadn't condemned another human being to death." I laughed a little. "That's real commitment, Darren. If it wasn't so despicable, I'd applaud your focus on the prize."

Each and every word hit him like a blow, exactly as I'd hoped. And finally stirred the desperate need in him to speak, exactly on cue.

"No, I didn't!" He shook, hands rising and falling, but again making no move to leave. "Yes, I took the slips, fine, I'm the thief. But I didn't hurt anyone. I didn't kill Halliwell! I swear." Sweat ran in runnels down his temples to his jowls, hands trembling, whole body shaking. His pulse continued to thud visibly in his throat, terror in his eyes raising doubt about my accusations. I'd been trained, after all, to read people and as much as I'd have liked to take out two crimes with one plant, I now suspected the killer was still at large.

Not that I was letting Darren off the hook.

"You didn't do anything to hurt anyone," I said, repeating his panicked assurance, knowing it was to the contrary. "Just ruined creators and their hybrids for financial gain." Yeah, okay, jerkface. If you say so. "No harm done."

He licked his lips, pushing himself forward from his lean into the boxes. Ah, here we were then. Darren prepping to escape was about as obvious as his attempt to brush over the facts. "Get out of my way."

"Not yet," I said. "Not until you tell me if Halliwell was going to out you or blackmail you." Darren's face twitched into sullen anger. "Blackmail it is."

"He already was," he growled. "He wanted more. I wasn't going to take the slip, I swear, but Halliwell demanded ten thousand and I didn't have it. I had a client who offered that much for the slip, so…"

"Two birds with one monkshood," I said. "You get to keep the ten thousand dollars and Halliwell…" I held both hands up and flat, tipping one sideways for effect. "Six feet under."

"I'm telling you," Darren was almost shouting now, trying to bully me back, gaining a little ground. He hadn't yet reached out, tried to touch me. Just let him try. "I didn't kill him. I have no idea who did."

"We'll see about that," I said.

"There's no we," he snarled then. "I'm leaving and you can't stop me."

"You're right," I said, stepping aside as the towering and truly impressive Cherise King entered the booth, her cuffs swinging from one hand, deputy appearing at the other side, just in case. "I meant *her*."

Did you really think after our last fiasco I'd try do to this alone?

I learned my lesson. And got to have fun doing it.

CHAPTER FIFTEEN

I joined Cherise as she slammed the door on Darren, the now terrified and begging rep slumping in the back seat of her Charger. His continuing attempts to profess his innocence in Halliwell's death came through muffled from behind the glass.

"I like him for it," she said. "He had access to the monkshood, obviously knows his way around plants, was being blackmailed—I'll find proof of that when we dig into his finances. Oh, and he knew where Halliwell's bottle was." All things I'd laid out to the man on the other side of the car door and yet none of which was actual proof. Circumstantial evidence or not, I had to relent on my lingering doubt.

"Pretty cut and dried," I said. "So, why aren't you happy, Sheriff King?"

She frowned toward the mansion proper, shaking her head. I wasn't the only one who had questions yet unanswered that rested uneasy in my mind? Of course not. She was ten times the investigator I was and if Cherise had doubts, mine were justified. "I don't know," she said, drawing out the words as though trying to come up with a plausible explanation for her misgivings and failing. "Something is missing, and I'm not sure what."

"Like the fact he wasn't the only one who knew where Halliwell's bottle was?" She nodded to that.

"It could have been anyone, Seph," she said. "Without his fingerprints on the bottle, or some proof he handled the poisonous plant, a lawyer could easily generate reasonable doubt in a case like this." She chewed at her lower lip, eyes narrowed. "And we might be missing the real reason he was killed. That just doesn't sit right with me." She shrugged then, headed for her driver's door, decisive in motion if not in thought. "I hate loose ends, and this feels like one giant unresolved question I can't tie into a bow."

I couldn't agree more, but the rest was up to her. I had no doubt we'd be discussing it at our next diner breakfast and likely weeks from now as the court case against him—hopefully it went that far if the DA agreed what she had was enough—moved ahead. For all I knew, more evidence would turn up or maybe she'd manage to get him to confess. Whatever the case, I'd be a willing ear to the unfolding drama because I was feeling more than a little invested for obvious reasons.

So nice of her to let me play like that.

I waved her off and turned, heading back toward the event space. Caught Jason Arnold watching and groaned softly to myself, knowing I was not only filthy and hot and tired but that I didn't really care what I looked like. If I smelled or needed a shower. Because you know what? I was very tired of being the target of his questions and false interest all for the sake of a story and the tragic ending that he likely only cared about because it sold magazines.

Tansy's plant wasn't the only fake around here.

"Talk to the sheriff," I said on my way by before he could open his mouth. And kept walking.

He didn't try to follow. Smart boy.

With the day's event over and extra security hired to patrol the grounds, you'd think I'd be able to sleep. Fall into blissful rest and the dreams of the just. Yeah, you'd think so. Since when did I follow normal patterns or let things go? Quiet dinner with the girls long over, even with Belladonna joining me this time, curled up at my feet and asleep herself, I found myself ignoring the fact I really needed shut-eye if I wasn't going to be a zombie in the morning. I sat up in bed instead, digging into this crazy plant world and all the people and players in this particular production, Cherise's loose thread mention making me *hmmm*.

Now, don't judge me for my lingering guilt that had me avoiding the obvious until I couldn't take it anymore. Yes, I looked into Jason, but only after I'd poked and prodded into the lives of the others. Thing was, I'd already disillusioned myself about his motives and chosen to put cynicism ahead of interest of a romantic nature. The good and mature and self-possessed thing to do, right? The independent woman who didn't need anyone, especially someone who had his own agenda. Still stung, I'll admit it. But I was far enough over his charm I felt I could be objective. Sure, I could, not a resentful or bitter bit of trigger seeking out more reasons to dislike him for playing me.

What was I saying about being mature about it?

It was finally curiosity that won out against

my disdainful attempt to write him off and eliminate any desire I might have had to uncover the truth I was sure I already knew. Couldn't leave it alone, though, could I? Had to poke the sleeping bear that was my ego. Called it curiosity when I knew in my heart it was really vindictiveness.

At first, his squeaky-clean persona irritated me. Surely there was something I could dig up to help in my quest to completely erase any desire I had to get to know him better, cut him slack. The fact I didn't find anything incriminating wasn't helping, the legit (if you could call a journalist that) reporter posted as the author of articles about Sandra, Halliwell, Pearl, even Lydia Powers. Not to mention countless others. I dug so deep into his past that I uncovered some rather out-of-the-box criminal reporting from his younger days when he worked for the *Portland Press Herald*. Impressive stuff, hard-core and dangerous, which begged the question, ultimately. What had driven a man who'd pursued drug dealers and murderers and corrupt politicians to write about flowers?

I could ask him, of course. But that would mean admitting I was interested in what he had to say, and I wasn't. Not even a little bit.

Sigh. Okay, fine. Maybe I *would* ask if the

opportunity presented.

Until I clicked through to his blog, the simmering jab to my self-respect I'd chosen to cyber stalk him while lying to myself about my motives no match for my remaining inquisitiveness. And found his most recent article.

Skimmed the contents. Anger growing exponentially. Each word layering over one another until I had to stop before I threw the computer across the room.

Blood boiling? You better believe it. And not in the way he'd been trying to inspire.

I simmered over "amateur hour" while gnawing on "poorly run excuse for an event" while I sullenly growled about "uninspiring presentations" before I slammed shut the lid of my laptop and snarled into the quiet of the room. If any ghosts had been present and listening, I'm sure I scared them away.

For her part, Belladonna woke to the noise, green eyes huge, pupils flaring to fill in the emerald until they were almost fully black. But, instead of running from me as I thought she might, she started up her engine, purring instantly rumbling as she stood and stretched. Yawned. Took her time as I watched and breathed and caught hold of my temper. She might not have been acting on purpose, with purpose (I had my suspicions about that), but she certainly knew how to gain attention and focus, exactly what I needed to calm the heck down. Her purr grew louder when she finally climbed my legs and settled with a hearty flop in my lap, head butting me for attention before gazing up at me in adoration, front paws making air biscuits until I stroked her tummy.

That only lasted a second before I cuddled her close, setting the computer aside on the end table, glaring at the machine like it was responsible for all that was wrong in the world. But no, not the laptop. I knew who the real culprits were. "Men," I said. "Who needs them, right?" Inaccurate and rather petulant, but that was my mood, so I ran with it.

She chirped her absolute agreement and murmured before settling in, her warmth and soothing purr the perfect interruption. Despite my lingering irritation and the need my brain had to replay over and over exactly what I planned to say to Jason when I saw him again, the cat won, bless her.

That now soft and steady sound carried me to sleep, my kitty's wet nose pressed to my cheek. I have no doubt, without her, if I'd been left to my own devices, I'd never have slept again.

Belladonna for the win.

CHAPTER SIXTEEN

My cat's soothing presence might have managed to score me a solid seven hours of uninterrupted rest, but she couldn't do much about the fact I was a dog with a bone and couldn't bring myself to let what I'd read go.

Should have, I'm well aware, of course, and the therapist in me offered up lectures and tools and choices that would have worked to my advantage if I'd chosen to step off and avoid any further upset.

Funny how knowing what's good for you, being trained for that very reason, and actually taking action on said best practices was the hardest thing to accept and enact no matter what excuses and intentions surfaced.

I had to be a sucker for punishment, right? Yes, I did. That's what had me checking Jason's blog the next morning before going down for breakfast. His newest post started out about Pearl Tolliver, the jerk, pick on an old lady like that. He was even less appealing to me now, imagine. His innuendoes about her being off her game, about her time off last year, poking into her family life and the suggestion she was having personal problems despite his utter lack of proof told me his brand of journalism bent toward the sketchy. Maybe that's why he quit real reporting. This kind of lazy and offensive suggestiveness without basis in truth wouldn't hold up at a real paper when lives were at stake. Of course, he'd fallen from grace only to end up writing about plants.

That's where he belonged. In the dirt. So much for openness and truthfulness and all that garbage he tried to foist off on me to convince me to trust him. Creep. He could take his sunglasses and nose booping and attempts to wheedle his way into my good graces and take a flying leap.

So there.

I found myself sniffing in derision. The fact he only posted his ridiculous and yet damaging speculation on his own private page and not linked or associated with the magazine he wrote for had me furious and judging him and ready for war when he made the terrible choice of crossing my path.

Full disclosure, all of that was awful, the things he'd written. But the real kicker, the trigger that had me so worked up wasn't about Pearl. It was the "knowledgeless helpers left to run the show" comment that really set me off, but if you want to quibble semantics, you can do it on your own time.

He did not just take a jab at me. He did *not*.

Oh, and his little mention about Sandra being dragged off by the sheriff? Failed to mention her return, didn't it?

I was wrong. There *would* be two bodies. But they'd never find his.

It took me about a half-hour to shower and change, to descend to the foyer and head for the dining room. In that time, you better believe I drew on every single process and healing technique and releasing tool I had to shift myself past raging fury and into calm again. Thing was, even I had my moments and sometimes just letting myself vent and fall into the kind of emotional overload I'd embraced was a good thing. Feeling it, letting it burn itself up inside me before I interacted with other human beings, was part of the growth mechanism. No way was I going to continue to let it rule me or ruin my day.

Which meant, through epic control, by the

time I landed downstairs, Belladonna long ago abandoning me for her breakfast, I reached the point of mostly calm and the acceptance that none of it mattered, certainly not the opinion or intentional bashing of one person out to forward his career no matter the consequences to others. Pity had replaced rage, not exactly an ideal emotion either, but I'd take it and the clear-headedness it happily provided me. Whatever happened in Jason Arnold's life to make him the way he was, I hoped he found peace.

Being the bigger person had its perks.

When I paused in the doorway to the dining room, Sandra smiling and laughing in the morning sunshine, my daughter chattering away in excited happiness, Thalia glowing in her very own sunbeam, I took a firm hold of what remained of my outrage and personal hurt—because that was all it really was, and I knew it, was still working on it—and set it aside in favor of putting this new day and the resolution of the event ahead of all else. Surely enough of what was meant to be a positive and growing experience had been ruined for them already. I was not going to draw any further attention to anything that I could do nothing about.

That saying about ignorance being bliss?

Made my bacon taste like ashes in my mouth no matter what I did, taking one for my particularly lovely little team and keeping the bubbling rant I continued to soothe with every tool in my arsenal. Small price to pay for the joyful trio and their willingness to carry on and finish what they started.

We strolled to the event grounds together, Calliope linking arms with me, smiling at me, cheeks tanned from the days in the sun, her golf shirt and dress pants a bit rumpled but come through about as well as the rest of this event.

"I'm sorry, Mom." She stopped me at the edge of the grounds, pulling me aside. "I've been wanting to say that for a while. Since, you know." She blushed, looked away. "I'm really sorry. You didn't deserve to be treated like that. You've only ever loved me and supported me. And all the things you've taught me have helped me so much."

I hadn't been expecting this particular conversation right now and was already emotionally vulnerable, in case you missed it. So, I had to swallow twice and blink a lot to keep from crying. She seemed to be on the same train ride I was, the pair of us holding hands and not speaking for a bit until I finally nodded, cleared my throat.

"I never wanted to be that mom," I said. "The one who used lessons instead of love."

"You're not," she said. "I swear. I don't know why I said that. Mom, you're the *best*. You always listen and you're always there for me." Calliope sighed deeply, squeezing my hands. "And I don't blame Dad. I know he loves me. He doesn't mean to…"

"Smother you?" Wow, that came out kind of harshly.

Again with the head shake of denial. "I don't feel smothered. It's just been so hard to be myself and keep it to myself. Not because I didn't want the two of you to know." She visibly struggled with the concept, though I was getting it regardless. "I wanted to be my own person without having to talk about it or have it cleared or bring it up to anyone."

"Independence," I said. "Callie, honey, you've always been worthy of it. You've never done anything that made me think you couldn't handle it. And I'm sorry if you felt like you had to overshare because of how we raised you."

"I trust you with everything," she said then, hazel eyes soft, heart open. "I don't know why I needed to know what it was like to keep secrets."

I shrugged, hugged her, then moved us along, ready for this day to be over so we could go back to our happy lives. "Testing waters is what it's all about, kid," I said. Winced. "That sounded so much like therapy."

She laughed. "It did. But you can't help it, Mom. That's the thing. You're not a therapist, it's not something you do. You *are* therapy." She hugged me and bounded off, full of energy and life and youth and I finally did have to turn away and cry a little because, darn it, she was a great kid, and I didn't fail her after all.

I kept my distance, both from Jason—who followed the judges all morning and barely threw me a nod—and the crowds, watching the last day of the event unfold as best I could from the perspective of an outsider. Yes, I caught myself a few times evaluating it from the point of view of a professional. Sure, this might have been a bit more organized or that could have gone a little smoother. But all in all, as the judges completed their rounds of the greenhouse and the competitors waiting for their final ruling, I came to one solid conclusion.

Thalia and Calliope and Sandra did a killer job. Yes, pun intended. Because even with a dead body, a plant thief and one of their sponsors dragged away and accused of murder, the three women I admired very much had not only held it together but carried on and were now concluding what I could only imagine would be an awesome ending to an event that would be even bigger and better next year.

I'd be out of town, by the way.

He made one effort to clear the air, Jason sidling up to me when the trio of judges, Calliope staying close to Thalia despite not needing to, stopped at one of the displays.

"This ends at noon," he said. "Lots of time for sitting tonight. And eating. And maybe a drink or two."

"I'm sure there is," I said, feeling my temper snap but proud of myself for holding it in. "Except, I'm sure there's someone a lot more knowledgeable you'd like to eat with. You know, so you're not bored," I threw some of his blog's words back at him, "with amateur conversation."

Jason winced. "You read my blog." His blue eyes flickered, regret there though I wasn't about to cut him any slack whatsoever. "You do know, like Pearl, my writing is all a show? Meant to sell magazines. Without controversy, there's no reason for people to pay and I lose my job."

"That would be a shame," I said. "I'm sure the *Portland Press Herald* was happy to see you go with that attitude." He started, surprise and his own hurt replacing whatever amounted to his attempt at regret. Yes, it was petty. Yes, it was beneath me. Yes, I said it, before I could stop myself. Done and done, so I moved on, knowing I'd berate myself and relive it in guilty instant replay later. "Enjoy the rest of the event. Or not. I really don't care which." I had to get away from him, my anger no longer fully under control. Which had me striding in the only direction available to me, closing in on Pearl as she spoke up about the plant she was inspecting."

"And I'm telling you," Pearl snapped at Sandra, "the layer of scent isn't nearly as delicate as it could be."

"Surely your nose is failing you, Pearl." The old woman flinched visibly at that, Sandra's confrontation stirring her anger. Was going around, I guess. "You've accomplished a wonderful combination here, Jane." She'd turned to the creator in question. "Well done."

Pearl scowled at Sandra's back as they moved on, hateful and certainly no show, though who knew with the experienced old judge? Until something twinged and, when we passed a display, I touched Pearl's elbow.

"Are these blossoms always this shade of blue?" I pointed to the plant next to me, Pearl's irritation at the interruption softening when she realized who spoke. She even stopped, observed the plant, touched the blossom delicately with one trembling fingertip, hand dropping instantly as she cleared her throat, the forbidden contact a secret between us.

"Always," she said. "Isn't it lovely?" Then carried on while I watched her go, gaze drifting to the deep green flower next to me.

And knew who killed Halliwell Thicket because Darren wasn't the only person whose secrets the dead judge had known.

Was he?

CHAPTER SEVENTEEN

I let the day wrap up. Again, I wasn't about to ruin the moment for the girls, not when they'd come this far. Instead, I hung back, waited with anticipation and regret, a text fired off to Cherise as the clock struck noon and the judges went to the podium to announce the final winners.

My sheriff friend arrived shortly after, and when I'd finished filling her in, she agreed to keep it quiet until after everything was over. Left the event and me to monitor the murderer, trusting me to do what was needed.

Because she was awesome like that.

I barely heard a word, clapped when everyone else did, didn't even really take note of who the winner was because, frankly, it didn't matter. None of it did, not while the real murderer smiled and handed out ribbons, her tiny body draped in a cardigan over her pretty flowered dress, the old woman's left hand shaking just a little.

Cherise reappeared right at 1PM, in plain clothes, just in time for Thalia's closing speech.

"I want to thank all our participants this year," the slim blonde said. "It's been an eventful three days." That met with some laughter. "And, while flowers can be dramatic, I don't think anyone expected this much drama." More laughter, everyone in high spirits. Murder and mayhem and mirth. Who knew? "Congratulations to our winners, and to those who didn't win. Because your efforts are the reason we're here. And will be back here again next year." That cheer was genuine, Thalia smiling and waving, stepping away from the podium to join Sandra and Pearl shaking hands with the prize winners still lingering on the stage.

"It's time," Cherise said. "How do you want to handle this?"

"Let her come to us," I said. "Thalia's having a dinner for the judges, so Pearl won't suspect a thing since the girls have no idea, either." This was going to break their hearts, but it had to be done. "Just, be gentle?"

"I still don't have proof," Cherise said. "I

did speak directly to the hospital and they told me she was admitted last year, though I'm not positive for what." Her hesitation faded. "If you're right, and I have every reason to believe you are, it all makes sense."

"I'm right," I said. "Here she comes." I stepped forward as the girls joined us, Thalia hugging me, then Cherise, Sandra even offering me an embrace before nodding to the sheriff. While I shook Pearl's hand, noting the soft vibration in her touch. I'd seen it over and over, but just in her right hand, not her left, the one she used to handle the flowers she wasn't supposed to touch. "Pearl, it's been a pleasure."

She smiled back, clearly excited. "I'm so happy to be back," she said. "How fun. Let's do it again next weekend." Her laugh had that youthful excitement of relief, of getting away with deceit and coming out the other end with no one the wiser.

Except, of course, I knew. And so did the sheriff.

"About that," I said. "Pearl." I stopped, couldn't go through with it.

While her face. Fell. Twisted. And she ran.

That I was not expecting. Not even for a heartbeat did I think the old lady would not only make a break for it but be able to move so freaking fast. In fact, she barreled past Jason, shoving him aside, the reporter stumbling out of her path with a laugh that turned serious when Cherise gave chase, me on her heels.

We didn't catch her until she'd circled the greenhouse, ran to the deadly garden and I knew—knew in my soul—what she had planned before stumbling to a halt, Pearl standing over the monkshood plant with her fist stuffed full of stems and leaves and blossoms. A fist she raised to her mouth in that palsied grasp.

"Don't come any closer." She panted, the dashing effort she made using up the last of her energy as she sagged to her knees. "I'll do it, I swear. Just let me die." She sobbed then, free hand punching her thigh. "It's over, it's been over for a year now and I don't want to live if I can't do this!" She spread her arms wide. "There is no life without this."

I approached her carefully, crouching, catching sight of Cherise while she drew near me with her hand on her gun but not drawing it, not yet.

"Pearl," I said. "You had a stroke. But look at you. You survived."

She snarled at me, clutching the deadly plant to her breast, hands filthy with the dirt she'd tugged it from. "You have no idea," she said. "Surviving isn't enough. It took *everything* from me."

"Your sense of smell," I said. Because with loss of smell came loss of taste. Which was how she'd been able to drink Halliwell's horrible concoction and not flinch. She nodded, weeping, silent wail making a rictus of her face. "And worse."

"I'm colorblind." She hugged the plant, rocking back and forth like she cradled a child. "Blue-green. My favorite." She hiccupped. "They told me I was *lucky*." That came out in a hiss. "That it was only minor damage, that I could live a full rest of my life." Her gaze snapped to mine. "They had no idea."

"You lost the two things you needed to do what you love most in the world," I said. "You're right. They had no clue what you'd lost."

She bobbed a nod at me, the plant so close to her mouth I barely breathed in anxiety she might eat it. Sure, if we grappled her and dragged her to the hospital, we might save her in time. But then again, how much would it take to kill a little old woman already suffering?

I had a feeling if that plant passed her lips, Pearl wasn't going to make it.

"I spent the whole past year," she wailed, "learning to compensate for it. And I thought

I could. But he *knew*." She rocked some more. "He knew and he told me he knew that night and he was going to tell everyone."

Halliwell. "That's the reason he wore that cologne," I said. "And the drink." The reason he smiled when she succeeded and won his bet. It only confirmed what he'd figured out. "It was to test you."

She shuddered, shrugged. "He wanted to ruin me just for the fun of it. So, I made sure he couldn't." She looked down at the plant in her hands, crushed and quite possibly already poisoning her. We had to hurry. "I knew about Sandra's little death garden. Came and helped myself to some monkshood. Squeezed just a bit of the root's juice into his bottle. More than enough." She petted the leaves, the flower. "I followed him then, the rest of the night, to make sure I gave him a sufficient dose." She shook her head at me. "You almost caught me, but I'm fast." That deep and sad sigh ended the fight in her. "It's so pretty, isn't it? Is it still purple?" The plea in her eyes had me nodding.

"Yes, the loveliest shade of purple," I said. "Pearl, please put it down."

"I *can't*," she said. "I won't go to prison. I'm an old woman."

"I'll make sure you have a garden, Pearl." Cherise's empathy vibrated in her voice. "Your very own patch to tend to. Minimum security, with a library. You can teach the other women to garden. It'll be a good life, the best I can offer."

She stared up at my friend, mouth gaping, eyes wide. "You would do that?"

"And I'll write a big spread, Pearl." Jason had followed us, the reporter's earnest offer making her perk. "All about your legacy. Everyone will know all about how brilliant you are."

I saw her hands sink, fingers uncurling, the plant dropping into her lap when she relented. Ignored the sound of Cherise calling for an ambulance, rushed forward, gently cradling the weeping old woman in my arms.

And held her while she sobbed over the loss of what had to be the only thing she ever really loved.

CHAPTER EIGHTEEN

I had just closed the door on Belladonna in her carrier when a text came through. I'd been expecting Cherise, the number unfamiliar, but the content told me exactly who was messaging me.

When you're ready to sit down for a bit, Jason sent, *I'll be here.*

Yeah, like that was going to happen. So why then didn't I delete his message and his number and forget about him forever and ever?

Don't judge me. A girl has to have her vices.

It helped that his latest blog post, live only an hour ago and it was barely 6PM, mentioned the event ending made up for the shortfalls and that the whole thing was saved by a clever blonde supersleuth who solved the murder.

He might get a pass. Eventually.

Cherise's arrival surprised me, the sheriff pulling up and parking next to me as the event grounds were already being disassembled just past the parking lot, the workers efficiently taking apart any trace of what had happened. By tomorrow, I had no doubt Sandra would have work well underway to erase all traces of the event.

While planning for the next one.

Did I mention I'd be out of town?

Thalia and Calliope emerged from the shrubbed path leading to the estate house, hand in hand as they headed toward us. I'd been expecting them and their hugs goodbye, at least, the opportunity for them to thank the sheriff and embrace her, too, just another bonus. Though, seeing them with Cherise triggered a memory from the night of the murder that had me wondering what Owen Graves wanted with my daughter.

I'd forgotten all about his odd behavior in light of everything else. And while I'd only just found fresh ground to stand on with Calliope and wasn't interested in adding tension back into our relationship, my silly brain now had something new to mull over I knew would get me in daughter hot water in short order.

Ah, well. Wasn't like she'd be shocked when I poked my nose into her business, right?

Leaving well enough alone wasn't my strong suit and she'd just have to learn to live with it.

Cherise interrupted the excuses my ego made for needing to know something completely irrelevant between my kid and the young man who acted as coroner, bless her. "I was going to call, but I thought I'd come over," she said, grinning at me. "Layla's still mad at me for putting an end to her party and I'm tired of listening to her complain about not trusting her." *Are you proud of me? I didn't look at Calliope or* anything. "Figured I'd deliver the news in person before I had to arrest myself." *Nope, not looking, not. Keeping my eyes locked on the sheriff. Snort.*

"Thank you so much, Cherise," Thalia said. "Is Pearl…"

The sheriff nodded. "I talked to the prosecutor and he agreed to go easy on Pearl. She's going to plead guilty in exchange for that minimum security I offered." *That was good to know. While murder was never something I condoned, neither was ruining the last chance an old lady had to cling to who she used to be. Yes, Pearl lied, I was well aware of that. Thing was, I didn't agree that her loss of smell and blue-green sight meant she was useless at the job she loved. The opposite. She worked even harder to be a good judge. And a killer. But that* was why she was going to prison.

Hey, I was never a fan of black and white, right and wrong, so sue me.

"Darren Moorehead, on the other hand, is getting the book thrown at him," Cherise went on. I'd said a sad farewell to Tansy, though she seemed optimistic that Darren's arrest meant she and her grandmother might have a chance with their next hybrid. Though I was positive he wasn't the only thief they had to worry about and wished them luck. "He's agreed to give evidence against his buyers, but I doubt he'll get much of a plea deal."

Sandra came trotting down the path, waving, beaming a smile at us, hugging Thalia in such a sudden show of happiness it had to be good news.

"I just got a call," she said. "Guess who's the new host of *Plants That Kill?*"

Thalia laughed, hugged her while Calliope groaned.

"Please get them to change that dumb name," she said.

Sandra beamed. "I'll do my best. And with Thalia's offer of help, her lawyers seem to think they can get my IP back. Which means all of the product ideas Halliwell stole from me might be mine again."

Oh, happy endings. They always made me

weepy.

"The thing is," Sandra said, hugging Thalia around the shoulders, "someone shared that talk you did and the producers are looking for an expert to help with the writing and research. Would you be interested?"

Calliope squealed for her, Thalia blushing and smiling while, as usual, my daughter's excitement was Thalia's excitement.

While my cat, wakened by the presence of people she couldn't snuggle, pawed at the driver's window and, the moment I opened the door, leaped down and took off.

Of course, she did.

At least I had four lovely friends to help me chase her.

Looking for more from Persephone Pringle? You're in luck! Book five, *Dead Over Heels for You*, is available right now!

ABOUT THE AUTHOR

Everything you need to know about me is in this one statement: I've wanted to be a writer since I was a little girl, and now I'm doing it. How cool is that, being able to follow your dream and make it reality? I've tried everything from university to college, graduating the second with a journalism diploma (I sucked at telling real stories), am an enthusiastic member of an all-girl improv troupe (if you've never tried it, I highly recommend making things up as you go along as often as possible) and I get to teach and perform with an amazing group of women I adore. I've even been in a Celtic girl band (some of our stuff is on YouTube!) and was an independent filmmaker. You can check out the whole Lovely Witches Club series for free at:

https://lovelywitchesclub.com.

My life has been one creative thing after another—all leading me here, to writing books for a living.

Now with multiple series in happy publication, I live on beautiful and magical Prince Edward Island (I know you've heard of Anne of Green Gables) with my multitude of pets.

I love-love-love hearing from you! You can reach me (and I promise I'll message back) at https://patti@pattilarsen.com/home. And if you're eager for your next dose of Patti Larsen books (usually about one release a month) come join my mailing list! All the best up and coming, giveaways, contests and, of course, my observations on the world (aren't you just dying to know what I think about everything?) all in one place:

https://bit.ly/PattiLarsenEmail.

Last—but not least!—I hope you enjoyed what you read! Your happiness is my happiness. And I'd love to hear just what you thought. A review where you found this book would mean the world to me—reviews feed writers more than you will ever know. So, loved it (or not so much), your honest review would make my day. Thank you!

www.ingramcontent.com/pod-product-compliance
Lightning Source LLC
Chambersburg PA
CBHW060943180626
46817CB00004B/1681